Vacation Piracy

A Novel by Mike Haszto

AuthorHouse™
1663 Liberty Drive
Bloomington, IN 47403
www.authorhouse.com
Phone: 1-800-839-8640

First published by AuthorHouse   12/12/2011

ISBN: 978-1-4685-0583-2 (sc)
ISBN: 978-1-4685-0582-5 (hc)
ISBN: 978-1-4685-0581-8 (e)

Library of Congress Control Number: 2011961608

Printed in the United States of America

Any people depicted in stock imagery provided by Thinkstock are models, and such images are being used for illustrative purposes only. Certain stock imagery © Thinkstock.

This book is printed on acid-free paper.

Foreword

You are about to embark on a journey. As a member of the brotherhood of the written word, I often toe the line between fact and fantasy, reality and creativity. A story is a story; whether we are telling it at the water cooler under florescent lights or around a campfire by the light of a warm flickering flame. Vacation Piracy? What in heaven's name could that be?

Before that can be answered in the next one hundred and eighty pages or so, maybe I should examine reality a bit...

What is reality and what isn't? In this day and age, it's become a challenge to decipher just that. In a time of 'reality shows' and sophisticated video games, the line between reality and, well, whatever we should call being across the line, moves. The line moves frequently. There are times that that line moves daily, and even with each experience by any anonymous person. How any of us can keep track of it often simply astounds me.

It used to be so simplistic. Growing up, we had reality and we had dreams. Since a vast majority of all of us didn't have what we wanted during our childhoods (speaking of materialistic things that only the rich kids would have), we were told to dream. And we were told that dreams come true. And when they didn't come true, parents, friends or whoever would look at you and say 'but you need to work hard at it and really want it for it to come true'. Um, yeah.

Of course, some dreams do come true. Growing up I wanted and wished so hard for the 1969 Amazing Mets to win the World Series. Ditto the 1968-9 Super Bowl III winners the New York Jets. Being a sports addict since birth with no other cultural attributes available, of course I had dreamt of such things. Of course, millions of others did as well. Maybe that's part of the equation...dreams come true with strength in numbers. Um, yeah.

For those of us who live through those types of dreams, the Mets and Jets have disappointed and destroyed any hopes and dreams pretty much since. Okay, there were the sold-your-soul-to-the-devil years of 1973 and 1986 for the Mets. Wash that away with the bitter disappointments of 1988 and 2000, and what have the Mets and Jets did for a boy (or a tremendous fan base) since? Hopefully, one gets the point. If not, I can start on a differing perspective to the same point with the New York Islanders and winning the Stanley Cup four consecutive years (1980-83) and hasn't come close to resembling much of a playoff team since…

Enough beating a dead horse. I'm sure the people of Cleveland have better examples since 1954…where their dreams of championships are now dreams of being even .500 for the season.

I digressed.

I remember the line between reality and dreams growing up were best illustrated by real life and cartoons. There was nothing like acting out Road Runner and Wile E. Coyote during a Saturday morning, huh? Or maybe Bugs Bunny and Elmer Fudd?

Of course, that line was sometimes obscured as well. How many of us went into school after watching The Little Rascals and mimicked some of their antics thinking they were for real? And how many of us had dreams that wanted Miss Magilicutty as our teacher…*that dream* never came true…

Our reality was still memorizing the multiplication tables and occasionally getting smacked with a ruler, a flying eraser or even a wooden pointer…

As we continued to age, video games made their way out to the marketplace to seize the attention of all of us. Some of us succumbed at the drop of a quarter while others wouldn't stray from their version of reality…

I remember taking vacation trips and prayed that they would never end. Reality or *Fantasy?* Could vacations actually be reality? Or is that just a week away from reality as we all wander into fantasy… Fantasy became the new buzzword as the childlike connotations of dreams faded into an adult world.

And in the adult world, it's certainly correct to think that reality has put the damper on fantasies and the kibosh on dreams for a great number of people. Bills, taxes, marriage woes that lead to split families, immaturity, laziness, government, working to support other LAZY people who aren't even tied to my family are just some of those adult reality issues. Of course, I didn't even mention hatred and crime and being held hostage by what happened hundreds of years ago...oh yeah, reality is such a trip for those of us who have to work our asses off to just keep our heads above water and maintain even a minute slice of sanity. Why can't adult life be as it was in our childhood dreams? I mean, I liked Willy Wonka, didn't everyone else?

Wow, talk about digression.

But one must admit that reality is no fantasy or dream.

And now as we moved into this century, reality shows popped up and pitted real people against real people in competitions. While people like me can only dream about spending a week in Fantasy World Camp with my childhood ball players of the Mets, Jets, or Islanders, there are reality shows that have swallowed up a great portion of television viewers around the world. Reality? Fantasy? What?

Of course, my dream is only a fantasy that will never come true. Why? Reality. Hmmm...was that an oxymoron I stated...or am I just the moron? Of course, my reality of finances bares out the reason behind my dream about living a fantasy will never be realized.

Reality shows? Are they reality? Or just another societal way of life for fantasies and realities that have evolved in such a way for our population that a dreamer like me has been left behind?

Look at those sophisticated video games. Now you can kill people for real and get away with it. So lifelike...so...reality? Not like my friend Mr. Coyote who died at least six times in each Road Runner cartoon...

I was amazed the last time I took a vacation down to Key West (another dream of mine that will never come to fruition for retirement because I will never be able to retire and I have been forever linked by unbreakable chain to Ohio against my will...that IS reality) that there were myriad ways of entertainment, much of it bordering on reality versus fantasy. I was stricken with some of the ingenious ideas of what some folks do to entertain the tourists. I guess I'm not the only dreamer.

For the record, I like reality. I also like fantasy. But I live for dreams. I cast my vote for mediocrity for the first two, because splitting time in reality and fantasy has its advantages. Some swear by it. 'Never take yourself too seriously' and 'it's not life and death it's only grits and gravy' come to mind as my two pieces of advice that I have received and still embrace today as philosophies. But dreams? If I could, dreams would be one hundred percent of reality. No pain, no suffering, only smiles and wide eyed happiness and peace. And at my age, there's a lot to be said about happiness and inner peace…two things I can only dream about because of my realities…

Another digression. No wonder my novels have so many subplots…

Vacation Piracy is a tale that I cooked up that sometimes skews that line of reality versus fantasy. Twenty two friends from all over the country go for a vacation adventure sailing around the Caribbean on a boat they captain. Sounds like fun, huh? You bet.

Well, it's not too long into the adventure that that's when the *real* fun starts…and somehow, it all goes wrong…reality? Fantasy? You make the call…

Jim Stowe embarked on such a vacation almost twenty years ago in real life. While this is in no way, shape or form any version of his actual journey, I felt I should give him credit for dreaming up this type of vacation and turning it into his version of reality. God bless you Jim, wherever you are today.

And a clearing of my throat…I do love living in North Ridgeville. It is the community type of living I have strived for. But DAMN this climate…

Enjoy the book!

Dedicated to Valarie Kage

Chapter 1

B eads of sweat were percolating from everyone's overheated body as they stood in the sun desperately trying to make heads or tails of what was unfolding before their overwhelmed eyes. Never in any amount of time would anyone ever think this possible. Yet, not only was it possible, it was actually happening.

Twenty two people consisting of couples and friends were witnesses on this steamy tropical day. Twenty two people who, when they awoke at the beautiful orange dawning several hours earlier, would have never suspected these turn of events.

Hunter James looked at his watch. From his touristy perspective, it might have been the last time that he could do just that.

"Hmm…just after ten in the morning" he thought to himself, "and what year is this? Two thousand eleven?"

He looked over at his wife Elaine, feigning a smile.

Her eyes held absolutely nothing back.

They were as wide and fixated as they could possibly be. One word came screaming from them: terror. The rest of her face was in complete rhythm as her eyes. Her soft cheekbones were somewhat taut. Her usually pouty mouth features were stern and deliberate. Her carefully manicured eye brows were disheveled. Although the rest of her face was in complete agreement, her eyes said it all…in high definition Technicolor.

Hunter again looked over at his mature pretty wife standing three people away from him and mouthed the words "what the fuck…is this Captain Hook?"

Suddenly one of the eight strangers who held control over the twenty two tourists grabbed Hunter and threw him across an open area and into a hard wooden wall. He crashed with his left shoulder and head hitting that wall simultaneously. He crumpled to the ground, also a very old hard wood surface, and lay there in an uncoordinated mess.

Elaine shrieked. The others were totally shocked by the sheer brutality as Hunter lay motionless.

The aggressor turned toward a few of the men who stood there stunned and egged them on…

"You want a piece of this? You want a piece of this?" he screamed as he waved his muscular forearms and biceps around.

There were no challengers.

Other than Elaine's cries and whimpers as she knelt over her husband, there was absolute silence.

Although, some would still swear that they could hear the percolating sounds of perspiration frying into a dry balmy salt on the skins of each individual. The temperature was well above ninety already at ten o'clock and the potential of zipping past one hundred was definitely a probable.

"Round these folks up!" were the orders barked by the leader who resembled a two century old pirate. His gray and brown hair was long and stringy as it flowed from under his hat to almost his ass. His skin was four shades and just as many textures past leather. There might have been three good teeth residing in his mouth…maybe. And his deep gravely voice was very convincing to the fact that he was the leader of this bunch of hooligans.

He carefully paced over to where a young beautiful woman was standing with her man and took his left hardened hand with the long curled fingernails and attempted to fondle the young lady's breasts through a yellow pastel tank top that overshadowed a petite pop-up style bra.

"HEY!" she scolded as she swatted the grotesque hand away from her chest.

He grabbed her by her long straight hair and strongly yanked.

She screamed.

Her dashing young husband took one step to intercede only to meet the point of a very long blade that was quickly released from its holster. There were ooo's and ahhh's from the captives in total surprise. The point broke the husband's skin in the sternum area and carved out a curvy bloody red line down to his waist, slicing through his white Florida Keys souvenir t-shirt.

Needless to say, he stood there frozen as a statue as the rich red blood formed along the line neatly carved.

"Another move and the wounds will go much deeper…"

The moment of terror continued for the group. It became obvious that this was indeed not a theatrical show of any kind. Yes, the massive yacht-sized boat of twenty two tourists had left Paradise Key just after sunrise. It was a rental paid for by Jim Stowe, a research and development expert who worked for a food industry giant, who was an accomplished sailing captain of more than twenty years.

His vacation trip of dreams was just a few hours old when this group of eight very hostile modern day pirates boarded and took immediate control of the boat full of tourists.

It wasn't as if no one could see them coming. After all, the pirate ship resembled just that, a pirate ship. There was no mistaking that. With its nineteenth century appearing sails and its even older looking hard wood structure, it was as authentic as it could be…right down to the black metal cannons.

All twenty two people had watched the ship approach from out of the west about two hours into their vacation journey of the Caribbean. And each one of them had thought the same thing: the ship was all just part of the touristy experience, with authentic looking pirates on an authentic looking ship that was meant to scare the bejabbers out of them.

It didn't take but a Florida second for them to realize that everything that appeared authentic actually was.

Let the terror begin…

Not one of the twenty two tourists moved much with Hunter James still lying on the floor of the boat and that carved husband of the beautiful young nymph still releasing droplets of blood. There were no challenges in the making.

The pirate captain turned back to the young woman and cleared his throat. He backed off of his original plan of fondling the woman for the moment, instead deciding that the present was the time for introductions and announcing plans.

"My name is Bones…Blackeye Bones. And make no mistake, we are pirates. We will do what we want…and we will get our way. We have no problems with pain, torture and killing. If any of you have any doubts, it's okay with us that you volunteer to be the first killed."

The terror that Elaine James had all over her face had now spread to each woman…and quite honestly, to each man as well. Captain Bones was quite persuasive in his introductions.

Following his five sentence announcement, he turned toward the young woman again and reached out for her breast. She trembled as he had his way with squeezing and feeling them, her looking freaked and scared toward her wounded husband.

"Very nice" he remarked, "though I admit I like a much larger and heavier breast. But yours are quite nice."

He turned away from his terrorized victim and paced toward the cabin of the yacht.

"Briggs! Carry on!" he ordered.

"Aye Captain" shouted a portly second in command identified as Briggs.

Three pirates went with the Captain. Four, including Briggs, stayed with the vacationers.

Time passed with tensions as thick as the salt air. Silence was the order for the moment. Elaine continued to tend to her husband Hunter, who was still lying on the floor slowly regaining consciousness. And the young lady who had been Captain Bones' momentary plaything, Karen, tended to the flesh wounds of her husband, Joe. Though the wounds were finely superficial, the terror felt was anything but.

Each of the couples held fast to their partners as the pirates guarded them in the hot, turning very unpleasant sun. And each person looked toward Jim Stowe as their leader and spokesperson to deal with this. The bottom line was he was the guy who organized this whole vacation trip.

As outspoken and casual as Stowe was as a person, he was a bit put off about approaching the pirates…especially after seeing what they did to his buddies Hunter James and Joe Mont. He certainly didn't want to say or do anything that would bring a violent wrath to his six foot five two hundred and twenty pound frame. He was willing to wait them out and ultimately see what they were going to do.

Time continued to whittle away with the sun slowly sliding from the east to overhead, and then toward the west. The course of the vessel appeared to be southerly, and the pirate ship followed the yacht close behind. The men stood still, each in deep thought about what the next move, if any, could or would be.

Another hour salted away with the group still in the same area of the boat, though the ladies were now sitting on the deck floor. A small heavily wooded island appeared off the front of the boat. It caught the curiosity of each person.

The silence was finally broken.

"Briggs, can you please tell me what the fuck is going on here?" asked Stowe.

"Shut the fuck up" he demanded.

"Briggs, at least tell us what to expect. The women are scared to death, and I imagine the rest of us are pretty close to that level. We've been standing here for hours. What's up?"

"Shut the fuck up" he repeated.

"Dude, I need an answer. My people are looking to me to figure out what is going on."

Briggs was unrelenting.

"Shut the fuck up."

"Briggs---what the…" began Stowe.

Briggs walked over to Stowe, who towered over the squatty Briggs.

"Hey mate, you better shut the fuck up. You wanna be the first one dead?"

"No Briggs."

"Well then, shut the fuck up."

Briggs brandished his long sword to Stowe.

"Don't make me use this…"

"Answers Briggs…I need answers. I am responsible for these people…" Stowe demanded.

"When the Captain wants to give you answers, then he will. Otherwise, shut the fuck up."

The agitation on Stowe's face was oblivious to Briggs. The others realized that their leader was about to blow like a volcano. Stowe's close friend from Bay City, Michigan, Alan Mayes, walked over to him and put his arm around his waist, turning him away from Briggs.

"Jim, let's not do something stupid here…" he said as he leaded him away from Briggs. "I mean, shit man, he has a gun and a sword here. You wanna be the first dead man?"

"This is bullshit, Al, and you know it. What the hell is this? Pirates on a pleasure sail? Two hours out of Paradise Key? Something very strange going on I these waters, man."

"Dude, I agree. But pushing these guys now may not be the way to go. I don't wanna end up like Hunter or Joe. Those guys are hurting…and frankly, lucky to be alive."

5

The frustration wouldn't pass. It gripped Jim all that more.

"Al, I've got twenty two people here who are crapping in their pants. I'm the one who brought everyone down here for this. I have got to do **something**..." he said firmly.

"What? Do something like what? They have guns and swords. And they look like they know how to use them. What does ending up dead do for all of us? Jesus, Jim, calm the fuck down dude...for all of us. Wait this out..."

Stowe turned back at Briggs, who was watching him closely. The two locked eyes for about fifteen seconds...serious 'I'm gonna kill you' eyes before Jim turned away. He surveyed his group of friends, who pretty much all looked the same...confused, puzzled and scared shitless.

Al said, refocusing Jim "I think the one thing you should do is make sure everyone is all right. We all look scared to death."

"You're right, Al" answered Jim.

He quietly walked away from Alan and moved slowly around the group starting with Hunter and Elaine, then moving toward Joe and Karen. All the while, he kept an eye on Briggs and any of the surrounding pirates...

Chapter 2

*U*nder the watchful laser-like eyes of the heavily bearded Briggs, Jim Stowe went to each of his good friends one by one for assurance that they were at least physically alright with the shocking turn of events of their vacation. It proved as therapeutic for Jim as it did for everyone else, as the normally stoic dry humor expert was a complete mess with vibrating insides that his outer shell hid considerably well.

He first went to Hunter James and his wife Elaine, a middle aged couple from the tiny hamlet of Lynbrook, New York. It was no stretch to understand that Hunter was still coping with the effects of his sudden crash into what felt like the immovable wall from the opening moments of welcome from Captain Bones and his merry band of troublemakers. While Hunter could still figure out where he was and who Elaine was, there were some missing pieces to his puzzle package. Elaine, normally a strong independent woman, was so spiritually distraught that she clung to Hunter like a child to a parent.

Any words Jim spoke to her were not received well, so he kept them brief. What did help was him sitting down next to the both of them and trying to reassure them by placing his arm around each person's shoulders, which then evolved into a touching hug. It seemed to work with Elaine more as he was very careful of putting any physical strength into a hug with Hunter knowing his hurting condition.

They both realized how deeply upset Jim was. After all, their journey to the sailing adventure was their first trip south to Paradise Key from the western shores of Long Island, also their first venture onto the water that was scheduled for slightly more than a week. Their friendship had grown to a robust forty some odd years, with Hunter and Jim first meeting during their childhood on Long Island. After sharing the joys of elementary school together, the Stowe family then whisked Jim away to the landlocked area of Blaine, Minnesota, where Jim had finished his childhood dreaming of sailing on the ocean.

This was Jim's second shot at captaining such a vessel on a vacation, his first with his group of friends. He and his wife Dyane are made from the same cloth, both loving the idea of sailing on the open seas, and had made their maiden voyage two years earlier as part of a small group of six, also leaving Paradise Key and taking a week to sail casually over the Caribbean at their leisure with nothing more than a map and a chart of the sea. Both were so hooked that they decided to do it again, this time with a larger group on a larger yacht. Fact is though, that this was Dyane's idea, and while sitting with Hunter and Elaine, it hit Jim like a tsunami of epic proportions…where was Dyane in all of this?

He couldn't believe that he tunnelvisioned himself into the turn of events so much that he lost track of where Dyane was. Was she even with the group when everyone was initially rounded up by Bones and his Mates? He couldn't remember seeing her at all.

He looked all around from his vantage point of the yacht's deck with an urgency that perked up Elaine.

"What's wrong Jim?"

"Dyane…where's Dyane?"

"Wow…I don't know Jim, I don't remember seeing her…"

"Shit! Oh my God…where *is* she?"

He tried to scramble to his feet but was quickly stopped by Alan.

"Not so fast, big man. Remember where we are?" Alan warned.

"Al, where's Dyane? Have you seen her?"

Although Jim was back in a seated position on the deck, the urgency increased exponentially.

"No, I have no idea where she is. She wasn't with us when they boarded. She must have been down below in the cabin."

"Shit! Alan! Shit!"

"What----the…"

"Bones is down there now" Jim concluded as he again tried to get up.

Alan stopped him again.

"I've got to find her, Al…why do you keep pushing me back down?" questioned a confused leader.

8

"Jim…how many times do I need to tell you? Look around. These people have swords and guns and obviously aren't afraid to use them. Think man!"

"But Dyane…"

"Yes, Dyane. I understand your need to find her. But do you wanna be killed before you lay eyes on her again? Let's hope that she's safe wherever she is."

"Al, that's not good enough. I need to know."

The six foot tall, one hundred and forty pound rail and his voice of reason was not anywhere close to winning this battle versus a six foot five and physically ripped individual.

Jim mustered a good part of his strength and fought through Alan's better judgment to get to his feet. His goodwill tour of his friends didn't get past the first stop as he veered quietly but well paced toward Briggs.

As he approached solo, Briggs grabbed for his sword and brought it about four inches closer to its freedom. His position was obvious to everyone standing there, except for Jim.

"Easy there Mate…you don't want to do anything stupid here…" was all that Briggs said in his gravelly deep voice.

"What exactly is stupid here Briggs?"

"Getting any closer to me would be very stupid, Sir…"

Jim halted his progress, still about ten feet away from a sword that was now about a foot away from being totally released of its holster.

"I'm not playing" Briggs warned.

"I need to find my wife" Jim demanded.

"Watch your tone. You're not in charge here."

"I need to find my wife" Jim repeated with the same tone.

"Watch that tone. Back down, Mate."

"I need to find my wife" Jim said again unrelenting.

"You need to back the fuck up" warned Briggs as he now let his sword escape.

The brandishing noise of Brigg's sword captured the attention of the other three pirates in the immediate area. They struck to the same defensive posture right away.

Jim didn't care.

He stood his ground with his arms out to both sides and again repeated his demand.

"I need to find my wife."

His voice was unwavering.

There was silence.

Jim again made his point.

"I need to find my wife."

Again silence.

It was more and more becoming quite the stand off.

Jim versus Briggs.

Big physically hulking man who was armed only with the strong desire to find his partner versus a chunky bearded and no so well oiled middle aged pirate who had one very distinct advantage. He was armed with a sword that would cut through anything with the cleanest of slices.

Neither was backing down.

There were no more warnings.

Everyone's attention was captured who was on the deck.

There seemed to be no solution.

Jim's eyes breathed like fire as he stood still awaiting Brigg's next move.

Briggs held fast like a championship poker player…attack or bluff, his face gave nothing away…

The silence was overwhelming, the waves hitting the side of the boat seemingly amplified because of it.

Then a sharp shriek pierced the silence. There was no mistaking that it was a woman in dismay. The only question was…was it Dyane?

Another scream ripped through the salt air with such force that it reverberated through the hearts and bodies of each of the vacationers on deck. The focus quickly turned from the standoff between Jim Stowe and Briggs to the cabin area where the two painful cries originated.

The passengers started taking inventory of each other as they needed to know just who the unlucky one in the cabin was. Was it Dyane, Jim's wife? Or was someone else with Dyane?

There was a good ten to twelve seconds of milling silence as everyone looked around. No one needed to tell Jim anything. He instinctually thought that it was Dyane. The fire in his eyes grew even more intense. Then again, the mighty sword of Briggs poised in the attack mode kept him from leaping toward the cabin.

Then…a third cry that pierced everyone again like a dagger. Each scream had no discernible words…just painful shrieks and howls.

Then…

"Oh my God…" stumbled a young lad named Dylan in a low defeated voice.

Everyone but Jim turned toward him.

"Oh my God…" he repeated.

"Oh no…" Alan Mayes rang true.

"Mandy? Where's Mandy?" Dylan asked, his voice now several levels past concerned and working straight up to hysterical in a hurry.

Jim shook his head.

"Oh no…" he said somberly.

Jim knew Mandy was with Dyane in the cabin below.

"Oh God, not them…watch over them…PLEASE" he thought and prayed in a split second.

Alan had the same thought simultaneously.

In that same instant, everyone on the deck said their own quick prayer.

Another scream put everyone's heart in their throats.

Jim had had enough. He reacted.

He lunged past Briggs, who took a swipe at him with his long sharp sword. He connected with Jim's side just below the ribs. It was obvious to everyone the slice was clean as a stream of bright red blood flew through the air as Jim hit the deck with a screaming thud.

He lay there for a brief second, blood flowing into his white polo shirt.

But he would not be denied.

He scrambled to his feet, right hand covering his new wound. He scampered for the cabin as quick as his weakened state would take him.

In that quick moment, the pirates left on the deck stood at attack mode surrounding the other passengers. Briggs watched as Jim raced to the cabin door, expecting him to eventually fall to the deck one final time. The trail of blood was all the evidence Briggs needed to come to that conclusion.

Yet, in this moment, Stowe was not to be denied. That is…until he hit the doorway.

He was met there by Captain Bones, who was holding a frantic and crying Mandy Dodge. The cherubic twenty year old with the innocent looks had torn clothes and a lot of skin showing, including a full breast. Between frantic cries she would catch her breath with sobering whimpers. His grip on her was one that easily created bruises that outlined a hand on her upper arms. Bones held her at knifepoint as well and came into the doorway with a face displaying happy amazement from finding and unwrapping a present...

"Hey Briggs" he shouted, "look what I found in a closet!"

Just as he came through the doorway, Jim tackled him and Mandy with a firm left shoulder, not realizing the knife that was pointed at her throat, or what consequences that would follow.

If anything, it was quite heroic...for the moment.

Bones went backwards hitting the door frame so hard that he almost tore the thing right from the sturdy hard wood wall. Mandy went flying past the doorframe and into another wall, eventually sliding down the wall and landing on her butt. Thankfully she hit the wall with her shoulders and back and not her head. Stowe drove Bones into the door frame, then veered off of him landing chest first on the deck falling short of the cabin wall. His right side was stained heavily in blood and whatever strength he had mustered up in his legs was now drained.

Captain Bones was caught off guard to say the least, flabbergasted as he tried to get up from his fierce collision with the doorframe.

Briggs and his men were frozen for an instant, then reacted by racing across the deck and poking two swords into the ribs of Stowe just above his bloodied wound. OUCH! Jim just lay there, half conscious and aware of what was going on.

"Shall we kill him now, Captain?" Briggs asked.

There was no immediate answer.

"Captain, I say we kill him now" Briggs rephrased.

Again, there was hesitation from Captain Bones.

The group of Stowe's friends were hushed over the heroic move of their leader, yet very concerned over his current condition.

In all of the confusion, Mandy snuck up to her feet and wandered away from the whole scene, reuniting with her new husband, Dylan. He immediately peeled off his t-shirt and helped put it on her, covering her victimized bosom. He held her as she alternated whimpers and sobs...

"I'm here, baby...I'm here...I'm so sorry..." he whispered gently.

She shook in his arms, at first uncontrollably, but eventually slowing the shakes down as her breathing slowed as well.

"Captain?" Briggs questioned. "Captain? Are you all right?"

Bones was still quite shaken up from his tackle into the door frame. What no one had realized was that a huge wooden splinter, about sixteen inches long and somewhat thick for a splinter, had penetrated the Captain's shoulder from his back side at a peculiar angle. Even Bones had no idea as he attempted to get to his feet.

Briggs took his sword out of Stowe's rib area and walked over to Bones. He tried to help him up, but Bones pushed him away.

"Kill him?" he shouted with a high strong voice. "Kill him?"

There was hesitation again with his command.

"Yes sir...shall we kill him?"

"Come on sir, I can kill him and throw him overboard...let the sharks have their way with him..." yelled Ratface, a very tall and thin pirate who was the ugliest of them all.

He stood over Stowe with the sword poking into his wound. It was as grotesque as one could imagine.

Stowe just stifled his reaction to all of the pain Ratface was causing. He didn't want to give that ugly son of a bitch the satisfaction of knowing just how much pain and suffering he was creating.

Bones still did not answer. He continued to pull himself up to his feet, now flexing the shoulder area that had bore the brunt of the doorframe. He still didn't realize that there was a wooden stake, if you will, sticking into and out of his shoulder. He garnered his strength again and screamed at Ratface...

"You want to kill him?"

"Aye Captain."

"You want to kill him?"

"Aye Captain."

For the third time, Bones repeated with emphasis on the word 'you'...

"YOU want to kill him?"

Not to be denied, Ratface screamed back licking his chops... "AYE CAPTAIN!"

"Back off Ratface...he is mine."

Chapter 3

"$\mathcal{H}$e is yours?" Ratface asked disappointedly. "Shit."

"Yes, he is mine...all mine" Bones reemphasized loudly.

"But Captain...why not let me have this one? He would be fun to carve up!" Ratface answered as he used his sword to carve out an imaginary person in the air.

"RATFACE! Back down!" demanded Bones. "I will not say it again!"

With that Ratface backed down from the hovering attack position he held over a bloodied and looking defeated Jim Stowe. He stood a few feet back of Jim and was at ease, laying witness to Stowe's sliced right side that was thoroughly covered in a deep red blood.

The wincing all over Stowe's face was all anyone needed to conclude that he was indeed done with any heroics for that instance.

Captain Bones made it to his feet and took a step forward, balancing his wounded shoulder and his dizziness with his left arm not far from the doorframe that had been so boldly hit by him a few minutes earlier. He also struggled to regain his form and still had no idea of the foreign body that intruded and protruded from his shoulder.

Bones held his position for another quiet moment when Briggs finally spoke up.

"Aye Captain, will you be finishing this varmint off now?" he leadingly asked.

"Aye" was his response, thought it was considerably weaker than his previous vocal commands.

Then without notice, Bones took a baby step forward with his right leg and tumbled hard to the deck. That sixteen inch or so thick piece of plank resembling a splinter on steroids was suddenly visible to everyone as he tumbled due to weakness. More importantly, the Captain's impressive sword went flying across the deck landing at the feet of Jim Stowe.

Stowe was in no condition to move towards it, but Scotty Mayes was. He was about ten feet away from Jim, and about fifteen or so away from Ratface. The angle in which the sword flew and landed spelt potential heroics for young man of thirty two. But was he up for the task?

Scotty had zero time to think. It was jump at it and see what happens, or it was stand still and continue on with this unique nightmare.

In grabbing the beginning of a deep breath, he lunged for the sharp instrument easily beating the reactions of Briggs and Ratface. He grasped the sword by the handle and lifted it in full control. He was surprised to feel just how heavy it truly was, but again, he had no time for analysis at this point. The control of the sword was his, no mistaking that.

His control lasted but a mere fifteen seconds. While surveying his options, a shot rang out.

Thud…clang…clang.

Everyone froze in disbelief.

They all turned left to see where the shot had originated. It came from behind the doorframe where Bones and Mandy had walked through earlier. The shooter couldn't be seen as yet, but whoever it was, it was clear that they were a damn fine marksman.

It was a single shot.

That's all that it took.

The sound of the thud was played by Scotty Mayes as he hit the deck with a finality. Considering a good part of his face and head was blown off, one could understand the finality aspect.

The part of the double clang was played by the sword of Captain Bones as it slowly dropped to the deck and bounced just once before settling down.

What a nightmare. People began to freak. There was screaming. There was yelling. People were running for cover. Chaos ensued from both sides. There were multiple bodies sliced up, wounded, even blown away…not to mention lying all over an area of the deck.

Briggs tried to restore order in the face of his leader being one of the bodies lying on the deck severely weakened by the overall happenings of the day thus far.

It didn't work.

Alan Mayes, Scotty's older brother, stood there horrified. All of the blood appeared to have drained from his face. He wasn't the only one.

Then, another shot exploded through the chaos.

Everything stopped.

Everyone looked toward the doorway to the cabin. They looked away quickly to see if anyone else was going to fall to the deck in fatal horror. In complete syncopation, the fraction-of-a-second look around the yacht brought everyone back to the place where the shot originated.

In a scene reminiscent of a swashbuckling Hollywood adventure movie, out stepped a gun toting pirate from the door way blowing the smoke away from the end of the gun.

This was no ordinary gun toting pirate.

This pirate was female…and a definite leader. Intimidation was an instinct. And she wore that well on her sleeveless sleeves. Her look was young and all business. Moreover, for those who didn't quite get with her way of thinking, the tattoos that ran up and down her arms of different pirate type hostilities and scenarios were convincing. The tattoos were colorful, though graphic, and continued across her shoulders and covered what could be seen in her front and back torso. Her legs were painted up as well.

While everyone else was quickly adjusting themselves to some sort of civility in the face of the surreal, she calmly walked over to Bones and assessed the situation.

"Damn men…" she began in a low tone while shaking her head, "good for nothing."

She reached down for the thick wood splinter that was anchored in the Captain's left shoulder area. She slowly moved it from side to side and top to bottom checking to see what the best angle for protraction would be.

Bones was oblivious as to what she was doing. He just lay there in painful agony.

She also looked over at where Jim Stowe was lying. The blood was puddling around his open wound.

"God, he looks just as pathetic…whatever happened to **real** men?"

she spun sarcastically. "Briggs! Go below and bring me some rags. Looks like I got some fixing to do!"

"Aye, Rusty."

Briggs motioned himself urgently past her and the Captain.

She screamed at him again.

"After you bring me those rags, look and see if you can find some needles and threads."

"Aye" he answered as he disappeared down into the large cabin area of the rental luxury yacht.

Up on deck, order was restored and the group of pirates was back in control. After witnessing all of the violence, not one of the vacationers had even a simple thought about doing anything heroic. They still had the fresh impressions of Scotty Mayes' death as convincing evidence to behave.

And after the entrance that Rusty had made into their lives, no one was sure to cross her…

No one.

She hovered over Bones, her muscular tattooed frame with the long ratty fiery hair intoxicating as well as intimidating. She seemingly played with the wooden chunk that was still lodged inside of the shoulder of Bones.

Then, with the ferocity of a lioness and the smooth velocity of a gazelle, she grabbed the thick chunk of wood and extricated it from him. No notice was given. One moment, wood…the next blood and screams.

"AAAAAAAAAAAAAARRRRGGG! Woman!" Bones yelled at the top of his lungs. "What the fuck, Rusty!!"

She grabbed the towels that Briggs had just appeared with and pressed them hard against his raging wound.

"Shut up you big pussy!" she laughed. "Ya don't shut up and I'll put her back…"

The vacationers all kind of chuckled to themselves with this unexpected show of comic relief. Not to say that it was comic relief, though, but who would have ever expected this to happen? First off, a female pirate, and secondly, one that'll blow a person away in an instant, and third, someone who would tell off the Captain? Call him a big pussy? And get away with that?

"Woman, how'd ya like to get that piece of wood buried inside of you?" Bones harpooned back at her.

"Like that would do anything to me? You're such a pussy. I shit stronger men than you everyday before breakfast…" she laughed in response.

Rusty surveyed the deck.

"I see you have this in control…" she laughed again.

She continued to press the towels firmly into his shoulder to stop the bleeding long enough so she could stitch him up. She looked around the deck again, this time in search for some alcohol.

"Briggs!" she bellowed "Go back to the ship and fetch me some rum and tequila!"

"Aye" he answered.

He hurriedly left the yacht for the pirate ship. Less than ten minutes later, he was back. Those minutes seemed to drag on forever for everyone on the deck.

"Dammit Briggs, you trying to kill him?" she wailed.

"No, Rusty, why?"

"Cuz you're slower than the mating period of two whales. Get your ass over here!"

He raced across the deck through the shocked, startled, and confused passengers to bring Rusty the bottles of rum and tequila. She grabbed them from him, quickly pouring some rum over the wound and then feeding some to Bones. She then took a huge swig from the tequila bottle and went to work stitching up his gaping mess of human flesh.

The screams were heard and felt throughout the boat. Fifteen minutes later, she rose from where Bones was now lying and stepped over to a very weakened and bloodied Jim Stowe.

She looked over his condition, then turned to Briggs and said, "Would you please get this body out of here?"

Briggs looked confused.

"Rusty, he's still alive…"

"Not him you idiot! Him!" she screamed as she pointed to the deceased Scotty Mayes who was a mere few feet away.

"Aye, ma'am."

"I can't concentrate with a dead body next to me…"

While Rusty poured the rum into Stowe's rib area, she again took another hit from the tequila bottle. Briggs and another mate disposed of Scotty's body over the ship's rail, and into the water. No one was happy about that, especially his brother Alan.

He quietly protested, knowing that any vocal moves from him could easily find himself the same way as his brother. Yet, with his subdued behavior and mannerisms, his message got across to every pirate as well as his friends on deck.

It took Rusty about ten minutes to sew Stowe's wound up and douse it with more rum. She dried the area up and positioned him also lying on the deck on his side so the wound was facing up. She looked around at the passengers.

"Is anybody with him? Wife…girlfriend?" she asked.

No one answered.

She became testy.

"Is anybody with him? Does he have a wife?" she yelled.

Everyone looked at each other, minimally stirring about. No one wanted to answer. No one knew how to answer. They were afraid to speak. Finally, Alan spoke up.

"His wife is missing. We don't know if she was tossed overboard by all the initial commotion or what. But that was Jim's issue when all of this happened. He was looking for his wife."

"How heroic" she said. "Ya can't blame a guy for looking for his better half."

She looked over at a group of women huddled together.

"Any of you know anything about taking care of wounds?" she barked.

"I'm in nursing school" someone spoke up shyly.

"Nursing school? Nursing school? What the hell is that?" she barked back.

"Training to be a nurse" she said with a shaky voice and a physical appearance to match.

"You have a name?"

"Summer."

"Well, Summer, get your ass over here and look after your leader. Care for him. If he needs anything, you have permission to let me know, and if I'm not here, let Briggs know. Got it?"

"Yes."

Summer walked slowly up to where Jim was lying, half conscious. She knelt over him and assessed his condition, then gingerly looked over at Rusty. Her look was a look of genuinely being scared.

"Look, Summer. I want you to look over him. Do not let him die. If he needs anything, help him. The same for Bones over here. You are to make sure these guys do not die. Understood?"

"Yes, ma'am."

Rusty then barked out directives.

"Briggs, you stay here. Razor, you come with me. Let's take a quick walk around this ship and see what we have here…"

"Aye" answered Briggs.

"Aye" vocalized Razor.

Chapter 4

S ummer went from leader to leader and did whatever she could in monitoring their conditions and nursing them back toward health. There wasn't much she could do except encourage. There was a large first aid kit available on the boat, but nothing to really help in dealing with primitive stitch jobs and the high possibilities for infections. Sure, there were ointments, but not enough for the dosages that each man needed.

So she did what she could while the other passengers just settled in during this display of peacetime. No one had any ideas what to expect. This trip, after all, was nothing that anyone could have ever thought would happen…ever.

Meanwhile, Rusty took Razor on a tour of the yacht. There was nothing out of the ordinary as far as size or accommodations or anything else. There were just twenty two passengers and their humble belongings… er…twenty one passengers now. As pirate booty was concerned, other than the boat, the passengers really didn't have much to offer she noted. It appeared that no one was of any status higher than middle class or slightly above, so Rusty's outlook was downright dour about extorting any money for their captives.

"Damn" she reacted to the thought that they would come up relatively empty on this takeover. "Guess we have some decisions to make…"

"Decisions Rusty?" Razor asked. "I'd say so…may I speak freely?"

"Kill the sarcasm Razor. What's on your mind?"

"My mind? Well, Rusty, for openers, we killed someone…" he opened.

"Yeah…that's what we do…" she lamented

"Yeah, but we killed someone…how many people have we killed in the past?"

"Okay okay, I get your point. Though, we have killed in the past…" she replied.

"Yes we have…under different circumstances. I have no problem killing…but…"

"But what?" Rusty asked sternly.

"But, what did he do to deserve that?"

"Are you questioning me Razor? You better be careful, Mate" she answered.

"I was speaking freely. I mean no disrespect, but killing innocent people…do we really need to?"

"Razor…we're pirates. We do what we want when we want. Obviously I need to remind you of that?"

"No Rusty."

"You another one getting soft on me? Don't any of you have any balls left?"

"It's not a matter of balls, and not being soft. Maybe just a matter of right and wrong."

"Right and wrong?"

"Yeah, right and wrong" he replied.

"What the hell do you mean by that? We are PIRATES! We are right, period! What the hell is wrong with you Razor? When did you get a conscience?"

"Rusty, you and I know that I'll always be a pirate. And I have no problems doing whatever we need to do to survive. Rob, hurt, kill…"

"Exactly! Rob, hurt, kill…" she interrupted "that's what we do."

"Yes…but an innocent guy? What did we gain from doing that?" he countered.

"We gained respect and believability. That got us what we needed. Now we can do whatever we want with them."

"Which brings me back to the original point. We have decisions to make" said Razor.

"Yes we do. But we need to check on the others. Need to make sure the Captain is okay…then we can go from there."

"Aye, Rusty."

They were gone no more than thirty minutes. The boat was sailing in the direction of a tiny island that was a long way's south of Paradise Key, where the rental boat was signed over to Jim Stowe and his crew of twenty one.

It was as beautiful a day as what possibly could be. The sunrise was a golden type of light orange with hints of a brighter orange and red, the antithesis of the adage 'red sky at night, sailor's delight, red sky in morning, sailors take warning…'. Well, then again, based on the current situation, maybe that old adage was correct indeed.

The twenty two friends, some life long, all met at the dock for the first time on the trip. All were on different agendas, coming by plane from as far away as Minneapolis/St. Paul, Minnesota and Bay City, Michigan and by car from as far away as Long Island, New York and Cleveland, Ohio. They were all on their own schedules, the only thing in common was meeting at five in the morning on Monday August 8th, at the docks in Paradise Key, Florida.

There were no cancellations from Jim's friends who were invited. He handpicked all twenty of his friends to accompany him and his wife Dyane on this adventure type of vacation around the Keys and the Caribbean. Jim, who had previously done this on a smaller scale, was so excited about his first voyage that he raved about doing a second with this group of friends.

Dyane was sold from the get go. She was an outdoorsy woman through and through. She loved camping, hiking, biking, you name it. And she always scoffed at those women that she would meet that whined about their own family vacations in the sand and surf of exotic locations like the Florida Keys or Cancun. They would complain about the sand, the hot sun, and the stickiness that would dominate their days.

Of course, Dyane would have none of that childish babying. She welcomed any time outside, whether playing golf in the rain or playing Frisbee in the cool sometimes frigid ocean. She was a captain of a mud volleyball team up in Blaine that played in summertime leagues. And she loved it with a passion.

Although Dyane and Jim didn't have any children, their zest for life and adventure kept them young at heart and soul. Moreover, they acted like children most of the time, without being childish. Their passion and excitement for most things were unsurpassed by anyone that they knew… or knew them.

They had an inner circle that they considered best friends. Most shared their visions of adventure, and it was those friends that they started their invitation list with. The list was from all over the country, as both Jim and Dyane were almost considered gypsies during their childhoods.

Dyane was the youngest daughter of an Army family, both Mom and Dad were career Army officers. Her childhood took her to several states, never really attaching any roots anywhere until she met Jim in college at the University of Michigan in Ann Arbor. Dyane went there because a couple of her close high school friends wanted to go there and she needed to get away from home. She was living in Pennsylvania attending high school at the time her and her friends decided on Michigan. Dyane was an easy sell to go there, mainly because Michigan offered pretty much the same climate and surroundings for her outdoorsy type of existence. One of her friends, Jessie Sherman, had some cousins living in the Ann Arbor area and had some connections to the university. And that's where she met Jim…

Jim spent a good portion of his teen years nomadic on Long Island, but also had residential stints in Cape May, New Jersey and Sandusky, Ohio, as well as stops in Minnesota and Michigan. He was not quite a basic jock, but more of an advanced one. He possessed size and strength much like a lumberjack. He was blessed with a scholarship offer to Michigan, and signed on the dotted line quickly. Playing football, he had a jock mentality in a jock body…but his demeanor was that of a good ole laid back country boy.

The two had met at a campus get together for freshman in Dyane's dorm. He was there as a guest of a team friend, and she was there with Jessie and her other friend from home, Chrissy. They somehow met over a glass of punch and the rest was an epic fairy tale of romance. Love at first sight both would say.

Jessie and Chrissy were both on their inner circle list of invitees. Both were in the same mold as Dyane: very beautiful independent women who loved the outdoors and had a great passion for life and living it. Their physical statures were almost carbon copies of Dyane: athletic on five foot seven or eight frames. The three were known for doing almost everything together when together, whether it was volleyball, snow ball fights, or drinking. Jessie and Chrissy, who both moved to Blaine after each's divorce a few years earlier to be closer to their soul mate Dyane, was on the boat.

Other inner circle invitees included Summer, who currently was watching over the injured Jim and just as injured Captain Bones, who was a nursing student and had come to Blaine with her Mom, Jessie Sherman, following her divorce from her father. She was a model child, student and daughter.

Hunter James and his wife Elaine were also on the boat, Hunter also nursing a nasty concussion from the original boarding fiasco that took place with the pirates. Hunter and Jim were childhood friends whose friendship only became stronger as the years went by. They had shared many experiences along the way…Hunter just as adventurous as and much more mischievous than Jim. Their experiences were always filled with two things…trouble and laughs.

Joe Mont and his wife Karen were also childhood friends of Jim from Long Island. They also kept in touch over the years, even though the Monts did eventually move down to Stuart, Florida for new career beginnings for Joe. Joe was a miniature golf professional who spent his summers touring up and down the east coast to play in events sponsored by the Miniature Golf Association of America. That all began on a simple little Putt Putt course on Montauk Highway in Islip, New York when Joe and his friends were all eight years old. Saturdays were free from nine a.m. through three p.m. and the parents would drop off their kids for an afternoon of fun each Saturday. Joe was blessed with talent and developed into one of the best trick shot artists of his time. The east coast was miniature golf heaven with several cities in several states known for their courses and tournaments. When Joe wasn't pocketing in the neighborhood of sixty grand during the summer months, he worked part time for the State of Florida in their transportation department doing road work. Karen was a part time model when not taking care of their two daughters. This was a family who thrived on the sun and the beach whenever possible.

Alan and Scotty Mayes were brothers who were also in the Stowe inner circle. While their big connection was golf, both Alan and Scotty loved the outdoors and always wanted to learn to sail. They also shared a love for the beach and the ocean. Their sense of adventurism is best told in their stories of how they devised their vacations. Each summer, while others would spent countless hours planning and changing their vacation plans, both Alan and Scotty would set the time aside, pack a gym bag of clothes for a couple of days, pack their golf clubs in the back of Scotty's truck and head in a direction. Every day, wherever they were, they would stop at each golf course they would drive next to and play eighteen holes. On any given nine day trip, they would play a minimum of twelve rounds. On most trips, they played at least sixteen rounds. Obviously improvised, no vacation was ever in the same city or ever played on the same golf courses.

Dylan and Mandy Dodge were close friends of the Stowe and James families. Dylan was the son of Chris Dodge, who went to school with both Jim and Hunter on Long Island. Chris and his wife both died in a car crash with a drunk driver several years ago on the Verrazano Narrows Bridge returning from Staten Island, and both Hunter and Jim were there to help and support Dylan in any way possible. He was a playground equipment salesman while she was a student at Hofstra University studying fashion design. Dylan and Mandy were newlyweds and this trip was sort of a delayed honeymoon for them. As of now, what a way to celebrate a honeymoon…

Rusty and Razor made their way back to the others on deck.

"What's the status of my husband?" she asked Summer.

Summer looked up at her, her red mane shielding the sun from her eyes.

"The stitches are holding well. He's still in a lot of pain."

"Treat him right for being so lame" she quipped.

"Excuse me, but may I make a suggestion?" Summer asked.

"What? Little pretty thing wants to make a suggestion?" Briggs chimed in playfully.

The other pirates made fun of her as well, especially the fact that Summer's voice was unusually high pitched. The chatter went on for a good twenty seconds or so with Summer just sitting there in silence taking the vocal abuse when Rusty put an end to it.

"That's enough! She has something to say…err…what is your name Honey?" Rusty commanded.

"My name is Summer. I suggest that we move both of these men inside to a bed where they would be more comfortable and out of the sun. Both are movable right now."

"You think we should move them?"

"Yes, it would make them both more comfortable."

"Your leader…what's his name?…is movable as well? He has a lot of my stitches in him too."

"Yes he is holding on fine. The stitches are fine. I'm just saying that both men would be more comfortable inside and out of the sun."

"More comfortable? We're not here to make things more comfortable" shouted Briggs.

Summer turned to Briggs and gave him a face that would kill. She let her aggression out.

"Look, you want two more dead bodies on your hand, that's your business. What's the point of stitching them up if you're gonna let them suffer and eventually die anyway? You all put me in charge of making sure they will be okay. Well, I'm telling you that they should be in a more comfortable way if they are to hopefully recover from their wounds. Those are *serious* wounds to both."

Rusty was impressed with Summer's outburst.

"Now that's a woman taking charge" she noted to all, shaking her finger at her. "Hell yeah!"

Summer gave Rusty the same deadly face.

Before Rusty could react, Summer chirped "Well, what's it gonna be? Move them or not?"

Razor drew his sword and pointed it toward Summer.

"You show respect to her."

"Easy Razor, put the sword down…" directed Rusty. "Summer, if you believe we can move them, then let's move them. You there…" she said as she pointed at Alan Mayes "come help move them. Razor, you help this guy move them down below, too."

And within a matter of five minutes, both Captain Bones and Jim Stowe were transported to the cabins below, to aid in each's recovery. Everyone else was directed to stay on the deck in the hot sun.

Chapter 5

The other passengers on the deck were very concerned for Jim, but really were confused in just how to react. The situation was quite unique and stunning. The shock value was still extremely high and being in the thick salt air and scorching sun only served to skew what was left of their perspectives on reality.

To summarize up to current time, Jim Stowe, along with his wife Dyane, led a vacation sail trip with twenty of their good friends, renting a tremendous yacht to freely cruise around the Caribbean. They met at the docks at Paradise Key "to be given the keys to the boat" at sunrise on Monday August 8th. Leaving the dock an hour later, their freedom was just two hours old when they encountered a ship of pirates.

It was a most unusual scene that took place not that far away from Paradise Key. They were just two hours into the trip and for the most part, no one even realized that there was a ship approaching them. Everyone was settling in for the cruise, most below deck checking out their accommodations and partaking of some beverages in a food/drink storage area. Jim, Alan, Hunter and a young family friend from Ohio, Brandon Logue, was all pretty much gathered at the controls with Jim at the wheel. The boat was steered toward the southeast and they were briskly moving away from Paradise Key and any signs of civilization toward the unknown. The four of them were sharing their dreams of adventure, well, at least their expectations of the trip. None of them were concerned about looking behind the yacht to see what they had left behind.

The terms 'amateur' and 'rookies' came to mind when thinking about how the pirate ship had appeared from out of nowhere behind them and had tracked them a good half hour as they neared the yacht. It wasn't until about ten minutes from the actual side by side boarding that took place that the pirate ship was even recognized. Talk about being in a zone. In the open waters, *no one* noticed a pirate ship, obviously not a normal looking boat in appearance, coming closer to them…*at ANY time since their launch?*

Who could blame them. They were all assembled for the adventure of a life time. So, they were unaware of their surroundings. Blame the adrenaline. Blame the testosterone. And, well, the trip of two hours was to live up to its billing immediately…it was to be an adventure of a lifetime.

In an intimidating show of just who was in control, there were confrontations of violence that left both leaders, Captain Bones of the pirate group and Jim Stowe of the vacationers, seriously hurt. Others in the Stowe brigade that were overwhelmed by hostilities were: Scotty Mayes, who was now bobbing with the barracudas after being mortally wounded by the gunfire of Rusty, the red haired wife of Bones; Hunter James, on the south end of a concussion when introduced to a wall on the yacht; and Dylan Dodge, who received a scar from chin to waist while coming to the rescue of his beautiful young newlywed wife, Mandy, who had been sexually assaulted by being groped numerously by Bones.

Rusty did some primitive stitch work on the gaping wounds of her husband and Stowe, who both were recently brought below deck to rest in more comfortable quarters. Summer had been monitoring their recoveries for the short term since Rusty's display of sewing skills.

One person was still unaccounted for in the Stowe party: his wife Dyane. Her absence actually triggered the first of the violent confrontations between pirate and everyday land lover. The last place she was seen was down below with Mandy as the ship was being commandeered by Captain Bones. Following Bones visit below deck, only Mandy was found by the crusty Captain, who unmercifully fondled the young woman tearing her clothes.

Ironically, Stowe was down below in the same area where his wife was last seen. There were several rooms down there, sleeping quarters that were available for the original twenty two sailors. To push that envelope of irony, Captain Bones was also down there in the same area.

But where was Dyane?

No one knew…yet.

Back on deck, several of the vacationers were wearing down from dehydration. The pirates surrounding them weren't generous with any food or beverage as one would expect, and a couple of the weaker passengers were showing signs of sea sickness. All of the excitement from the morning no doubt contributed to the feeling of collectively being beat down.

Alan Mayes assumed a leadership role in the absence of Jim Stowe. He wandered slowly over towards Briggs, who was left in charge as Rusty went below to tend to Bones.

"That's far enough, Mate" Briggs warned in breaking the silence.

"Briggs, how about some water for us?" Alan asked.

"Sorry, do you see any?" he responded salty.

"Come on Briggs…water…I know you know what that is. We need some…" Alan pushed.

"No. Settle down and get back with the others" Briggs pushed back.

"Briggs…you're not listening. We have people who are weakening fast. We need some water. I'm not asking for control of the ship back. Dammit, I'm requesting some water" Alan grumbled most audibly, not taking Briggs 'no' or his saltiness for an answer.

Briggs stood his ground silently.

"Goddammit Briggs!" yelled a frustrated Alan.

Alan made a move forward and Briggs jumped back into an attack stance.

"Last warning, Mate! Don't!" screamed Briggs.

"BRIGGS! Water! We need some NOW!" Alan screamed losing control of his temper.

Briggs stood like a statue, continuing to aggravate his confronter to no end.

Before Alan could make his next move, two eighteen year old boys made their way to the area of the standoff.

"Briggs, what's the deal with this?" Brandon Logue intervened loud enough for anybody on the boat to hear. "You know we are weak. You know we need water. You know we have water. Yet, you won't give us any water. Why? What's your deal, dude?"

The other teenager, Mark Russell also from Ohio, answered his friend "Hey man, he's just being a dick."

Of course, Russell's comment could be heard by Briggs as well as everyone gathered in the area. Briggs turned and looked sternly at Logue and then Russell. He was not amused.

"We can all see that he's being a dick, Mark. What I want to know is why? There's no reason for him to be a dick. He's got the weapons. We don't. We're just thirsty."

Again, Logue's words could be heard throughout the boat, including the cabin area under the deck. The confrontation captured the attention of Jim Stowe, Summer who was attending to him, and Captain Bones and Rusty who was for the moment caring for him.

The vocal insults flew again when Russell simply deadpanned in response "Dude, they're pirates. Pirates are dicks. That's their job. Don't you remember reading about them? Come on Logue."

"But there's no reason for this, Mark. They already captured us. Game over. What's the point in weakening us? What's the point in killing us? They already have our stuff. Dude, like I said, it's game over."

It was almost as if these two were putting on some theatrical event. Both had made their way up to where Alan was confronting Briggs. It was stage-like, so to speak. Both were unusually very loud, as if they were purposely projecting their voices to everyone on the yacht.

But to the casual observer, it also appeared as though these two boys had a death wish…or at the very least was pushing the irritation factor with Briggs and company.

Briggs stayed silent and at attack attention mode.

"Game over? It's not game over. They're PIRATES! Their game has just started. It's about punishment. It's about suffering. It's about torture and then death. It's not just robbery and you're free to go…" ranted Russell.

"Shit. Yeah, I guess you're right. But we still need some water! Briggs, how about it?"

Briggs stood tall. It was time for another pirate to jump into the action. Ratface walked over to young men and grabbed a hold of each with a hand and screamed at them.

"Both of you get the fuck out of here. Go back to the others and shut the fuck up!"

Ratface shoved both of them back in the direction of the others. They both fell to the deck temporarily and jumped back up to their feet.

"All I wanted was some fucking water…" Logue said in disgust.

"Fucking pirates…" Russell added.

"You got a problem little boy?" Ratface screamed at Logue.

"Yeah…all I want is some fucking water. We all need some fucking water."

"Sounds like you need to get some water. SO what's the problem?" Ratface chided in egging him on.

"You have the water and we don't" answered Logue abruptly.

"So what are you gonna do about it?" challenged Ratface.

Logue went silent.

"Come on little boy, what are you going to do about it?" Ratface challenged again.

Logue was no more than six feet from Ratface. The tension was incredibly thick. They went eye to eye, both shooting laser flames at each other. Though, Logue still stood there like a statue. Was he succumbing to Ratface? Or was he plotting his next daring smart mouth move?

Ratface was not going to give in. Pirates don't ever do that. So the pressure was on Logue. Was Logue calculating? Or was he scared out of his mind.

"Just as I thought…gutless…" Ratface stated while lowering his eyes. "What a fucking pussy."

As Ratface turned to begin walking away from Logue, Logue finally attacked. He jumped at him and then tackled him. He didn't really catch Ratface by surprise, but the sheer strength that Logue displayed brought Ratface down in a tumble with the much younger Logue.

They rolled on the deck, with each combatant taking turns of being on top and controlling the tussle. Logue used his raw strength and sizable weight advantage to gain control at times. Ratface used his long arms and wiry size…also his massive bad breath to gain control in his favor at times.

A crowd gathered around the two. Pirates mixed in with the group in curiosity as to how it would turn out. No one left disappointed. Action was plentiful: from fisticuffs to Logue's specialty of kicking in the balls. Both fighters spared no energy or focus. They went at each other and both realized that it was going to be a fight to the death.

Logue was quite impressive and the match was even for the first few minutes.

During the initial tumble and rolling, the belt of Ratface that was holding his sword and knife broke free, landing the weapons about twelve feet away from the action. No one in the crowd moved toward those tools of human destruction.

And Mark Russell, one of Logue's best friends from Ohio, stood very concerned and wanted to jump in to help, but hesitated in fear of another pirate backstabbing him and ending his life in a fleeting moment.

Alan Mayes looked over at Briggs and flatly pointed out "all this for some water. Feel good about yourself?"

Briggs took the challenge posture to Mayes. Mayes didn't care. He had nothing to lose. He didn't back down and prepared himself for a rumble as well. He wasn't planning on making the first move, but was solidly in position for a counter attack.

Meanwhile, Ratface got an upper hand on Logue as he grabbed an unidentified object made of metal and smashed it into Logue's mouth, pieces of teeth and streams of blood going airborne. He hit him again literally flattening his nose across both cheeks.

In a last ditch effort before realizing that death was at his door, Logue reached and grabbed for the crotch of Ratface. The blood curdling scream that spanned five pitches from deep and dark to high and breathless signaled a direct hit for Logue. He squeezed those nuts until they almost ripped away from the rest of its belongings. Both hands were holding on for dear life as Logue couldn't breathe. All anyone could hear were the deafening shrieks of a maimed Ratface and the slurping sound of Logue attempting to breathe.

Ratface dug deep one more time and smashed Logue's face with all the strength that he could muster. While still holding that cylindrical metal object, he crammed it into the nose area again of Logue, this time ripping his nose right off of his face. The exposed sinus cavity was quite the gruesome sight, several onlookers turning away in fright and terror.

With that move, Logue lost the grasp on Ratface's scrotum. His arms went limp as though his source of energy was just unplugged.

The second of the vacationers had just died. This death was over some water that they needed badly.

As Logue went lifeless in the arms of Ratface, he turned away and curled up in a fetal position writhing in pain.

At that moment's notice, Mark Russell leapt from the crowd of disgusted onlookers and jumped on top of the unsuspecting Ratface. With one brisk and juiced up punch perfectly placed into the crotch area of Ratface, all was over.

And just as quick as that move was, Russell regained his feet and ran. With three pirates closing in quickly with guns drawn, Russell headed for the nearest railing.

The guns went off in a hail of one way gunfire, the sounds muffled in the sea breezes though heard nonetheless. Russell continued his run away at first somehow avoiding being hit by the bullets fired upon him in retreat.

More gunfire sounded the continued aggression as the pirates closed in on him. And then with one wailing cry, Russell jumped into the air hitting the railing like a gymnast on the horse. He made contact with the top of the railing trying to use it as a springboard into the water.

As he made contact with the rail, the cry indicated that he had been hit, a splat of blood splashing through the air in slow motion for those who doubted the shot's accuracy. With one leg, he barely touched the rail. With the other, he hit his mark perfectly, springing himself sideways over the rail and into the warm waters of the Caribbean.

The pirates raced over to where the jump took place, shooting aimlessly into the water. They shot their pistols until there was no more ammunition to be shot. They stood there scratching their heads believing that there was no way for him to survive such a gunshot and a fall into the water from about eighteen feet.

As the ship continued its path southward toward that island, there was no sign of Mark Russell anywhere. There was no head bobbing. There was only the splatter of blood indicating a hit.

Chapter 6

The ship docked alongside the pirate ship in a secluded little inlet on the south side of the island. The island wasn't large by any standards and it certainly was a departure from anything that had been charted previously by mapmakers. Outlined with seemingly rows of palm trees of all sizes…well…palm trees and palmetto trees, it easily resembled a small island of jungle behind the tropical trees.

There were hints of civilization the closer the ships docked in that isolated harbor. There were no modern day concrete and steel docks, though there existed a home made good old fashioned wood dock that wasn't very impressive. It looked old, worn and torn…splintery and rough. Quite honestly, it looked like a perfect traditional pirate dock. Bright green moss seemed to glow as it grew all over the lower half of those docks.

The water in the harbor was see through…like a water color sun dress with the sun shining brightly behind it at the right angle. It was enough to be jaw dropping. One could easily say that hundreds if not thousands of fish were schooled all over that harbor. And, anyone could attest that there were dozens of species of fish as well.

Because of the narrowness and shallowness of the harbor, the boats needed to set anchor about a half mile from shore. The mood on the boat was that this setting of anchor just might be the last that this yacht was ever going to experience. By the time the ships had set anchor and the people occupying those ships made their way into the smaller row boats the pirates used, it seemed as though a quiet depressive spell was cast.

The little inlet bay was just barely that long to begin to keep the ships somewhat secluded. There were no islands that were visible to the naked eye in any direction, giving everyone that much more of an isolated feel. It was eerie, but then again, after losing three of the original group of twenty two during the first few hours of this misadventure, eerie had already become passé.

Only eighteen of the remaining nineteen de-shipped. It was a somber stream of humanity that made it into the smaller row boats for the forty five minute trip to the shore. Of course, they had to row those boats as well.

Several of the captives were having serious issues with their strength. They were permitted to sit while the others rowed. The rowing turned into a blisterfest pretty quickly, but no one else was available to take over the rowing duties, so the first set of rowers had to stick it out for the whole journey to shore. The boat was so quiet in human volume that one could hear the fish smack up against the sides of the boat.

Upon reaching the shore amongst the three foot waves that helped guide them, several pirates came out to help carry Bones to shore. The waves from the tides made him weaker, causing him to vomit three times during the ride in. Conversely, Stowe had a bumpier ride with less attention, but held up much better than his leadership counterpart. While decidedly severely seasick, he kept what cookies he had inside of him. One of his personal pride statements that he was trying to adhere to was to not show weakness in the face of adversity. Stowe was very much a motivator and an inspiration to the people he came in contact with. There was an air about him that screamed 'the ultimate leader'. And he believed that living by that credo in particular was priority important.

Stowe was also carried to shore by several friends, knowing that it was vital to keep the sea water out of his stitched wounds as much as possible. Jim was so focused on his pain and wounds that he completely lost track of Dyane. Of course, having Summer by his side helped immensely to deflect his focus from the absence of Dyane and closer to dealing with the pain that enveloped him. And it was only Summer who truly knew what Jim's physical and mental condition was. She felt that no one else needed to know at present, that there was enough concern about their own welfares to occupy their time.

By the time everyone had made it to shore, there was no confusion or identity crisis concerning who was in control of things. The posture of everyone involved gave any doubters their answers. The pirates were walking tall and broad. The vacationers were hunched over and walking gingerly and slow. They appeared to be beaten down in status and hope.

Rusty clung to Bones' side as he was transported to an elegantly looking home, tropical in nature, that was not quite a quarter mile from the beach and on the outskirts of what seemed to be thick jungle shrubbery. Bones also had another female that was walking along side his carried body. She was somewhat younger and looked like a close version of Rusty, sans the wrinkles and the leathery skin. She had the eyes of Rusty, the same type that could make one fall in love in an instant with her...yet in that same instant could shoot daggers right through one in a cruel mean slaying.

She was eighteen or so and on a frame of five feet ten inches, she looked considerably overweight in an athletic way. She was the daughter of Bones and Rusty, and no daughter of theirs would ever be plain fat. Yes, she was thick, but she carried it well. Her name was tattooed across her shoulder blades, just below her somewhat long thick hair. It read *Jewel.*

This was her first appearance to Stowe's weary group. Her unique beauty caught the eyes of the travelers, and the sharp tongues of two college girls who had attended the trip out of Paradise Key. Eryan Bangs and Gianna Anthony, both college friends of Summer Sheridan from the Minneapolis/St. Paul area suddenly had a mouthful to say after remaining absolutely quiet up to this point.

"Who the heck is that?" wondered Gianna.

"She ain't all that" critiqued Eryan.

"She ain't all what?" asked Gianna.

"She ain't all that" repeated Eryan.

"I don't know. She looks like she's pretty hot to me!" stated Gianna with a smirk.

"She ain't hot. She's a pirate."

"Sounds like you're a little jealous..."

"Jealous my ass. She's a flipping pirate. What don't you understand?"

"I understand she's a pirate. Big deal. I'm just saying she's cute for a pirate. Anyway, you think she wants to be a pirate?"

"When did you come out of the closet?" Eryan smarted off.

"What are you talking about? Like eeeewww. Get serious" Gianna spouted dramatically. "We talk about girls all the time."

"Not pirate girls..."

"Nope, not pirate girls. But I'm just saying..."

"Just saying?"

"Just saying she's cute."

"She's not cute, she's fat like me..." said Eryan, a college volleyball player and ex-softball player.

"You're not fat and neither is she…" Gianna argued.

"You can say that because you're the skinniest thing on the face of this earth. You turn sideways and you disappear. God Gianna, you make Taylor Swift look like a pumpkin."

"You making fun of me?" accused Gianna, who really was a college swimmer.

"Always" blasted Eryan with a smile.

"Anyways, you are a jock. You're supposed to be heavier. I just swim. So I'm naturally skinny" philosophized Gianna. "That Jewel chick is bigger than you, but she's got a cute face. She just does. Her eyes and smile remind me of Kate Hudson."

"Kate Hudson is as skinny as you. How can she remind you of Kate Hudson?" asked Eryan.

"Her eyes and smile, dumbass…not her body" she stated rather bluntly while giggling.

Eryan laughed.

The two girls had finally come out of their shell of shock from the morning takeover. Strange conversation as it was, it continued. While the topic was still Jewel, they discussed about meeting her and picking her brain to find out what it's like to be a pirate girl…and of course if that's really what she wants to be.

The girls were best friends with Summer, who was still by the side of Jim Stowe.

While Rusty and Bones sheltered themselves from everyone in the confines of their residence, Summer and Jim were set up outside on a summer-resortlike lounge chair about eight inches up above the sand. Summer's main concern for Jim now was to keep the sand away from his fresh wounds. Considering the soft breezes blowing and that sand pretty much is everywhere, it was a formidable challenge.

There were no real quarters for pirate prisoners. There was no housing, and no yard with a barbed wire fence. It was pretty much a casual situation with armed pirate guards in a designated area on a corner of the beach. Since there were really only two places to run if there was an escape (jungle or beach to water and swim until eaten by a barracuda or shark), there wasn't a great worry about such an escape.

Alan Mayes, self proclaimed leader while Jim was recovering, was still very much subduing the tension and stress that overcame him while dealing with Briggs over water. Mayes was a ticking time bomb and the group could sense that he was going to blow very soon. That was very unusual for him, but seeing the stress erupt with having a front row seat to his brother's murder, as well as to all the violence, murder and mayhem since, one could understand why he was behaving as such. He nervously kept an eye on everyone around him, especially Briggs. He sensed that he could very well be next and there was no way that he wanted to end up like his brother, Scotty.

Upon arriving on shore, Alan helped guide everyone together to the area that Briggs had designated. With Ramon, Razor and two other burly looking ugly pirates guarding the captives, Alan made sure that each captive was alright for the moment. He chatted with each one about keeping their behavior and he went on to say that only he should get upset with Briggs or any of the other pirates. He talked about the need for no more loss of life. Each prisoner understood. Each had had time now to get their emotions back into control.

So Alan took it upon himself to revisit his conversation with Briggs. He was cautious.

"Hey Briggs…when can we get some water?"

Briggs just looked at him, acknowledging him physically, but appeared to ignore him verbally.

"Come on Briggs. Why this hard ass act? You already have captured us. You've won. We all need some water. Come on, Briggs" he pleaded.

Briggs stoic posture began to weaken. His rigidness began to soften. Without saying a word, he turned and walked away from Mayes toward the series of houses that were clustered together off the beach. His pace was a normal one, no sense of urgency and no sense of wasting time. He disappeared in the direction of Captain Bones place, but Alan couldn't be sure.

A few brief moments wandered by and Summer disturbed the trance that Mayes was in.

"Alan, Jim wants to see you."

Alan snapped out of the funk he was in as he watched Briggs walk away. He looked over at Summer and smiled.

"Yes, right away. How's he doing, Summer?"

"Actually, he seems to be doing better than I expected."

"Okay, that sounds good. But exactly what do you mean by 'better than expected'?" he asked.

"Well after seeing what we saw on the boat, I thought for sure he was going to slowly and painfully slip away."

"I can understand you thinking that. This certainly has been a tough morning to swallow. Who would have ever thought that this would happen?"

"And Alan, considering the type of medical treatment Jim received…I mean, come on, do you really think that he has a chance of survival?"

"I can only say yes, hope for the best and pray a lot. I'm not ready to lose my best friend. I wasn't ready to lose my brother. But I did."

Alan stopped suddenly, his eyes tearing up.

"I mean, what the God damn hell is going on here? How does something like this happen? WHY does something like this happen?" he let loose.

Summer reached for Alan, brought him close and hugged him.

"I'm so sorry Alan…I'm sure we are all very sorry for what happened."

It was a small gentle and tender moment amidst an ocean of chaotic life turned upside down.

They both walked through a small maze in this area that was mainly open but also possessed a storage shed and small building that presumably housed prisoners.

The storage shed had a variety of tools and functional equipment that was used on boats. It reeked of the sea and dead sea life and seemed to nest billions of sand gnats and horse flies as well as a variety of sand spiders and other creepy crawlies.

"Eeewww" Summer commented as they walked by the insect nests.

"Yeah, make a note for all of us to stay away from here…" Alan dryly stated.

The small building resembled a large bunking area, with wooden shells for bunk beds. There were five of those units that could sleep ten on hardwood slabs. There was no sign of bedding and no other rooms such as a bathroom or shower area. It was void of all other furniture, just an empty room with those five wooden bunks.

They also strolled through several areas of palm trees as they approached the long wooden lounge chair that Jim was lying on. He looked mighty uncomfortable, but the good news was that he was awake, conscious, and alert. Alan shook as his body showed the reaction to how Jim was lying there helpless. Amidst a background of paradise, the scene was anything but just that.

"Al…how are you and the others?" Jim whispered as he reached out with the arm from his good side. "Come sit for a second."

"Jim, my God, look at you. We're all fine…the ones who are still with us…"

Alan's eyes teared up again as he looked at Jim.

"Al…the ones who are still with us? What do you mean?"

"We lost a few of our group, Jim. How much do you remember?"

"What? Who did we lose? You mean…separated from us right?" Jim asked as his whispers became frightfully louder.

"No Jim. I mean, they're lost…gone. What do you remember?" Alan emphasized.

"Remember? I remember getting slashed by some pirate. I remember charging another and smashing him into a wall. That's it. Where are we?"

"Jim…grab my hand. So much has happened."

Tears ran down the faces of Alan and Summer as they tried to remain calm and in control of their emotions.

Jim reached for Alan's hand. The fright seemed to leap from Alan and onto Jim.

"Tell me, Alan. Tell me what's happened."

"Jim, it's not pretty. We've lost three already, and one is still missing."

"Lost three? Al, what do you mean?"

"Jim, they're dead. They're gone."

"What???!"

"They're dead Jim…they were killed."

"What? Oh no! I can't believe this. Oh my God. Why? How?" Jim asked.

All the weakened calmness that Jim possessed was now squandered. He shifted to frantic quickly.

"Jim, calm down. You can't bring them back. We've got to get you strong again. We need you with us" Alan said.

Summer leaned over Jim, then knelt and leaned over and tried to comfort him. She helped to slow his breathing and Jim pulled himself together somewhat. He adjusted himself at an attempt to get more comfortable, but the stitches and the oozing from the wounds made that almost impossible.

"Al, who did we lose?" Jim questioned.

"Jim, are you up for this? We can cover this later. You really need to rest and get stronger" responded Alan.

"Al, I need to know. Please. I am a shattered person right now. I need all of the bad news now so I can work through it as I rest. I assume I will need all of my energy in the future."

That you will, my friend, that you will" said Alan.

"Well, Jim, we are on some island south of Paradise Key. No idea exactly where, but we must be at least ten miles away. There is no sign of any other islands around us. The eighteen of us are in a pirate camp, I guess one could say. Yes, we are captives. Now what that all means, I don't know. Hell, I can't even get us water."

"Water? They won't give us water?" Jim queried.

"I've been trying to get water for hours."

"Everybody else okay?"

"Jim, so far of the eighteen who are here, you are the worst off. Hunter has a bad concussion it seems and Joe has a bunch of sword marks all over his upper body, but he appears to be better off than you. He has no stitches, while you my friend, have way too many to count. I think we are all in agreement when I say, it's a wonder that you are still with us."

"So we were boarded by pirates for real?" Jim backtracked.

"Yeah...it's real."

"That in itself is hard to believe."

"Trust me. The dead are dead and your wounds are fresh and painful. This is no dream" Alan replied bluntly.

Alan's tears had ceased at present, though Summer's were still releasing with regular rhythm.

"So Alan, please tell me...who is no longer with us?"

"Your two friends from Ohio, Brandon and Mark are dead. They were in a fight with a pirate in support of my confrontation with Briggs over getting some water. Brandon stood up for me and took on one of them."

"He did? Wow..."

"Yeah. For a while it was pretty even. But the pirate got the upper hand and messed him up good. When Mark witnessed that, he jumped in and finished the job on the pirate. To save his life from three pirates, though, he ran and jumped off the ship while getting shot. We never saw him again."

"So he may be alive?"

"We don't think so. We know he was hit, we saw the blood splatter while he jumped. And that jump was about twenty feet high into the water…filled with sharks and barracudas. Open wound, blood, sharks, you can finish the thought there."

"But he was a college swimmer…"

"Jim…his head never came up. The pirates looked for him. They must have shot over twenty times at him on the boat and then in the water."

"Oh."

"Yeah."

"Who was the third one?

Alan took a deep breath and tears escaped.

"Scotty" he sputtered.

"Scotty? Oh Alan…I'm so sorry."

"Yeah, Scotty. They shot him."

"Shot him?"

"Yeah, right after you went down."

"Did you see who shot him?"

"Yeah."

"Which one?"

"I think her name is Rusty."

"Her?"

"Yeah. It's the Captain's wife."

"Oh my God. Alan."

"Yeah."

Jim brought Alan down to him. The three of them just hugged and prayed that this was all a dream. But Alan and Summer knew better…

Chapter 7

The afternoon wandered by like a butterfly floating on a breeze. The general consensus was that everyone was so worn out from the morning festivities that a siesta topped the agenda of priorities during the late afternoon hours. Just about everyone took a couple hours for a power nap. Soon afterwards, it was time for another type of power.

With everyone on island time, meaning no one really knew what time it was, nothing really seemed as it was. The captives kind of floated in and out of consciousness as the shock from earlier wouldn't shake through their systems quite yet. The pirates all went through their afternoon routines in their village, but the seven who returned to land who were involved in the ship raid were not seen. Most were sleeping. But it was anything but quiet inside the home of Captain Bones and his wife Rusty.

"Alright Bones, what are we gonna do with them?" asked Rusty with concern in her voice.

"I don't know. Kill them for all I care" answered Bones.

"We ain't gonna kill another eighteen people. Stop that shit right now."

"Rusty, what do you wanna do with them? Release them? Just rob them, kill three, and then release them? Hey, they killed Ratface. I mean, we are pirates, right?"

"Honey, we don't have enough food and water to keep them here for more than a day. What were you thinking? What was the plan? Eighteen hostages? Eighteen prisoners?"

"What do you suggest?" Bones pushed.

"I don't know...I don't know. We took on more people than we have in the past. After killing three, we can't just let them go…but we haven't killed twenty people before…" answered Rusty.

"Let's do this" suggested Bones. "Let's make them survive on their own. Separate them. We'll take the hurt so they can get better. We'll keep the men out in the bunk area tied up and we'll keep them guarded. We'll take the women and divvy them up between the pirates and make them earn their keep keeping house and doing chores."

"Interesting Bones…interesting. We've never tried this before. But how would they eat? We don't have that much food around."

"I'll tell you what. Make them hunt and get their own food…" replied Bones. "Some can fish in the harbor; some can go collect fruits in the jungle."

"What's the long term plan? Spend their lives here?" asked Rusty.

"I don't know. Give me some time to think. My shoulder and head are still killing me."

"Well, I don't wanna push you here, but I think it's important we figure this stuff out as soon as possible."

"As soon as possible? What's the rush? We have control. We have the power. We can intimidate and break them down. After they've been broken, we can do anything we want. Their survival depends on them, not us. If they have the will, they will find a way to survive. Then, in the meantime, it gives us time to figure out exactly what to do with them… make them pirates, go after ransom, who knows…"

"Make them pirates? What?"

"How do you think pirates have sustained themselves from generation to generation? Sometimes we need to replenish ourselves with some outsiders that we have broken down and then built back up in our ways…"

"What? When was the last time that ever happen?" laughed Rusty. "I've never heard of such a thing. Brainwash a prisoner to be a pirate? HA!"

"Just keeping the options open, hun…" he smiled, then winced, through the pain.

"You are insane, do you know that?"

"That's what keeps me sane! Being insane!" again laughed Bones.

He winced in pain again.

"Alright, you rest. I'll get the wheels in motion."

Just then, there was a knock at the door. Rusty went and answered it. It was Briggs.

"Sorry to disturb you."

"What is it Briggs?"

"They are still demanding water."

"Demanding?"

"Well, no longer demanding like on the ship. Now it's more like pleading."

"Pleading? Like begging?"

"Yeah, I would say so."

"Briggs, take five people at a time, lead them to the sea. They can have all the water they want. When they are finished, take five more. Do not take five men at the same time. Mix up the people. I don't want them to overpower you and Ramon."

"Yes, Rusty."

"And make sure that at least three others are guarding the rest of them. I want loaded guns and swords on everybody. Got that?"

"Yes, Rusty."

"And Briggs…stay tough on them. Do not soften up. We are pirates, we have the power, we are in control. Got that?"

"Yes, Rusty."

"Good. When they are all done with this water business, come back to me and I will tell you how we will separate them."

"Yes, Rusty."

Briggs left the Bones house and headed back to the prisoner area. On his way, he rounded up Ramon and Silly Willy and headed for where Alan and Summer were…right next to Stowe. R-Tard was guarding the captives along with Razor.

"R-Tard…status report?" asked Briggs.

"All is qw-qwiet wight now. Over half of them awe s-s-sleeping either on the wood or on the floor…" he said in his strongly accented stuttering voice.

Briggs looked over at Razor.

"What did he say?" asked Briggs.

"All is quiet and okay sir" Razor said with a grin.

"Good…and it better stay that way" grinned Briggs. "R-Tard you stay here and guard, Razor, you and Ramon come with me."

The three pirates shifted their positioning over to where Alan, Jim and Summer were.

"How's he doing?" asked Briggs to Alan of Jim.

"Weak at best but hanging in there. Do you have an answer on water?" Alan kept his answers brief.

"Water?" repeated Briggs.

"Yeah. Water" Alan replied.

"Yes I do. Get your group together. Put them in groups of five. No more than three men in a group. Let me know when you're ready."

"Ready? Ready for what?" asked Alan.

"For water."

Briggs walked away. Alan stood there scratching his head.

"We need groups of five for water?" Alan asked himself loudly.

Summer shrugged her shoulders. Jim just looked off into space. Alan did the same, but he wasn't in the same universe as Jim. He continued to pace a couple of steps and turn, a couple of steps and turn, over and over. His wheels inside his head were running hard and fast, but were getting nowhere.

Summer broke the trance.

"Shall I bring the others over?" she asked Alan.

Alan snapped out of it.

"Yeah, I guess" he said.

"Okay, be right back."

Three minutes later, the sixteen others who remained all stood in a semicircle around Alan and Jim.

"What's the good word?" Hunter James asked. "God knows we need a few of these."

Alan scanned the group.

"First, let me tell you…" he began. "We all don't know each other as well as everyone knows Jim. I would suggest that since we have all encountered this adventure together; let's get to know everyone here that's left. We all need to band together if we are to get out of wherever we are alive. And whatever it takes to support each other, let's do. Second, we have seen and lost friends, and brothers, by doing heroic but rash moves. Support each other. But by no means, risk any more life. They have demonstrated to us that they will kill us. So please, whatever we have to do, let's make sure the eighteen of us leave this place together and alive."

"Amen brother" Hunter interrupted.

There were echoes of "Amen" and "yes" from the group.

"Finally, we will break into groups of five. They told us that if we want water, they will take us in groups of five. We can't have more than three guys in a group. I'm not entirely sure how or what they will do to us, but we aren't in a position to piss them off any more. So, Joe, you and Karen pick three more. Hunter, you and Elaine pick three. Dylan, you and Mandy pick three. If there are any left, which there shouldn't be, they can be with Jim, Summer and me. I suggest we do this, and everything else, quietly. Do not draw any unnecessary attention to yourselves. They are watching. Any questions?"

Everyone was silent and just shook heads no.

"Okay, then let's get into groups. If they want us in groups for anything else, stay in these groups."

There was some milling about, but within sixty seconds, groups were formed.

Alan signaled over to Briggs that they were ready.

Briggs, Ramon and Razor trudged over to the groups and led the first group from the prisoner area.

"Follow me" Briggs told Hunter.

The group followed the pirate down the beach to a special area of the shoreline where the clear warm waters were washing up onto what appeared to be a pristine shore. It was a quiet part of the inlet, undisturbed in beauty.

Hunter's group looked puzzled. Each were wondering why they were led on some island beauty sightseeing tour when they were under the understanding that they were going for water. Each stood there confused as they looked at Briggs and the other two pirates.

Briggs returned the favor, looking at them strangely as well.

"Well?" Briggs broke the silence.

"Well what?" Hunter replied.

"Water" Briggs pointed down at the obvious water.

"Yes, water. Can we get some?" Elaine jumped into the cryptic conversation.

"Right there" Briggs motioned.

"Right where? You mean here?" Hunter questioned and pointed down.

"Yes."

"Oh. We were expecting a sink, a faucet…you know…water…" Elaine muttered. "Any cups at all?"

Briggs, Ramon and Razor looked at each other. A few seconds later, they broke into laughter.

"Cups?" Briggs said in laughter.

"They want cups?" Razor laughed even louder.

"Ramon, show them the cups" Briggs said, then erupted in laughter again.

Hunter's group just stood there watching the humiliating show put on by the pirates. Yes, they all felt stupid, and were getting aggravated the more these three laughed at them. Hunter's head began to throb as he was witnessing this mockery.

Ramon walked up to Elaine, grabbed both of her hands unexpectedly, and put them together in front of her. He made them for a cup.

Elaine was horrified.

"You want water?" Ramon shouted. "This is how you get water."

Ramon himself cupped his hands as he knelt on the sand at the waterline. He scooped his hands into the clear water and brought them immediately to his face. He repeated the motion several times, slurping some water as well as smearing his face with quite a bit as well. He looked up at the captives.

"Water. Comprende?"

"But, isn't this salt water?" Hunter asked Ramon. "We need water, not this."

Ramon looked at him with lasers protruding from his eyes.

"Look, you want water or not?" he said rather irritated. "This is not your rich America. This is all you got. Drink up or not, I don't care."

They all looked at him in disbelief. But they all came to realize quickly that they had no choice. It was all starting to sink in, this whole day that turned over their lives. They had no choice.

Hunter was the first one to drop to his knees and demonstrate what needed to be done. He slurped up a handful of water, like he tasted something for the first time.

"Hmm…this tastes like water, not bad…not bad at all…" he critiqued.

He slurped up quite a bit more. Looking up at Elaine and the others, he grinned.

"This doesn't have that salty taste at all. Fascinating. It's hard to believe, but this actually tastes like water."

Hunter cupped his hands some more and splashed his face and hair, washing some of the perspiration salt from his skin.

"It's nice and warm, but not to warm. This really feels refreshing. Elaine, trust me, this will make you feel better."

He then stood and helped each member of his group in kneeling on the sand and watched them get water. Not a word was said by Elaine or the rest of Hunter's group. They just did it. While they did, Hunter tried to get Ramon to discuss the surprising water taste with him.

"I'm really shocked that this isn't salt water here. This is part of the inlet, and the inlet is salt water. Ramon, can you explain this?"

Ramon just looked at him in disgust.

"Briggs? I mean, really, I can't believe this is water..." he went on.

Briggs didn't offer an explanation as well. Ramon was pissed that Hunter didn't show the intimidation of being in control of pirates. It was more like he was having a conversation with some friends over a beer or two on Long Island. Briggs also was confused by Hunter's sociability.

Finally, he just came to a conclusion himself and spoke aloud "must be a natural spring feeding this area..."

When they were finished taking multiple turns, they were led back to their designated area. Then it was the group led by Dylan next. They repeated the process, complete with disbelief and realization.

The Joe Mont group followed. Same drill, same results.

Alan, Summer and Jim slowly made their way over. It was the first steps Jim had taken since his tackle of Captain Bones on the boat. He walked cautiously, still in intense pain and hunched to one side. Summer helped to guide him with Alan.

When all was done and slurped and the groups were back together, Briggs took Alan and Jim aside and laid down a few laws. There was no bathroom, so bathroom breaks were in nature...one at a time with a pirate standing within twenty feet or so. Water breaks came at designated times by the guards. Briggs told them that they were going to be separated the next day into how they were going to live there for the current time, and that they would all sleep together for that night in that little shack with wooden slabs for ten. He also warned them to be careful of the insect life. They were big and they bite painfully hard. He suggested that no one sleep on the floor overnight, as most of these bug creatures hunted their food during the darkness.

Briggs told them that there would be more information tomorrow and he would answer any questions they had now.

Alan, in his usual dry way of speaking, made a couple of points.

"Guess release is out of the question..."

Briggs looked at him and gave back some of Alan's dry sarcastic wit. He pulled out his sword, showing it off.

"I guess killing you is out of the question..." he said with his gravelly voice "...for now."

Alan swallowed.

"Briggs, what about food?" Jim asked wincing. "I imagine we are all hungry to a point."

"We will discuss that tomorrow."

"But we haven't eaten today" pounced Jim.

"Tomorrow" Briggs answered sternly.

Jim was visibly shaken by the answer and his position.

"Anything else?" Briggs asked.

"Guess not" Alan replied.

"Good."

Briggs walked away, taking Razor with him. Ramon stayed with R-Tard and a couple of other pirates, standing guard.

As nightfall dropped on the sleepy little island with the secluded area of life, Jim and Alan spoke about myriad things...brainstorming and analyzing what their position was and what, if anything, that they could do to improve on it.

The sleeping arrangements were made without issue. Fitting eighteen people on ten bunks wasn't difficult, though it was a bit of a challenge. There was no privacy amongst the prisoners. Yet, they all dealt with their current situation as best as can be expected.

Dreamland was indeed peaceful for the group. Thank goodness.

Chapter 8

*A*ctually, all was not as peaceful as one would have imagined.

Jim had quite the nightmare and woke up screaming for Dyane about an hour before sunrise.

With his impaired mobility, there was nothing that he could do. Everyone with the exception of Summer stayed in a deep slumbering sleep. Summer tended to Jim, trying to keep him as calm as possible. He was a sweaty mess, and the one thing that she was afraid of was beginning to happen to Jim. His body temperature was so up, the perspiration a big clue, but combined with the clamminess and the heat coming from his head, she knew fever was setting in. The end of that equation usually meant infection.

Jim went through some rough shakes at times, but Summer was successful in keeping him as calm as possible and eventually rocked him back to sleep. It didn't take her long afterwards to join dreamland once again.

Sunrise on the island meant everyone was awakened from their needed sleep. Yes, everyone woke up. Yes, everyone was still on the island sleeping next to each other, some sitting up, some curled in fetal positions spooning another. But it was sleep.

The emotions were drained. The output of said emotions was far too great to withstand yet a second day. So, everyone awoke with blurry eyes, trying to rub the reality from them.

It seemed as though the brainwashing tactics of the pirates were just the breaking down process they needed with these prisoners.

Sunrise was anything but quiet. There was a group of pirates making all kinds of noise as they loaded a couple of boats to go out on another mission. Ripper and Tibs were now watching over the prison camp, and they made enough noise with metal trash cans to awaken islands three miles away.

Ripper grabbed Dylan and Caleb from their sleep and dragged them to a group of pirates who were taking supplies to a boat.

"Let's go…and don't say a word" Ripper demanded.

"What the ----…" Caleb sounded off.

Ripper gave him a rib punch that took his breath away.

"I said don't say a word."

Dylan initially struggled with Ripper and he gave him a rib shot as well.

"What the fuck!" he screamed back.

Ripper hit him again.

"Get yer asses over there and load that boat!" commanded Ripper. "Yer both going out to get food for your camp."

Both were feeling the effects of those punches and slowly moving toward the group of pirates who were loading one of the boats. Their lack of urgency didn't set well with Ripper.

"God damn assholes! Any faster and you'd be going backwards! Now get yer asses moving!" he screamed as he kicked Caleb in the ass.

They were loaded and out on the boat within ten minutes, and along with another boat were headed to the larger ship docked in a secluded part of the inlet.

The rest of the group milled about trying to get their initial focus on the day. It didn't appear as any of the weary travelers were habitual sunrise risers.

Following a couple of hours of waking up and getting water, Rusty, Jewel and Briggs came into the camp area and met with Alan, Jim and Summer. Jewel was holding a canvas bag with unidentified items inside.

The rest of the captives were strewn about the beach within their designated areas, all deep in thought about what consequences were waiting in front of them. They all looked strung out, with their newly bright vacation boat clothes looking a bit dingier and out of place. Then again with all that they have been through, they absolutely looked out of place to begin with. Nary a smile was present. The little conversations that were happening were all quiet and full of worry and concern.

Jim was feeling a little better than during the night, though the fever slightly worsened. The sweats and shakes had subsided for the time being though he wore his discomfort all over his face. The usual poker face and dry wit similar to Alan's was most definitely not his strong suit the past day or so…

Rusty reached out with the first olive branch.

"I hope you're feeling a little stronger today. Let me look at that. I want to make sure it's healing right."

Jim was a little taken aback by the greeting.

"Uh…okay…sure."

"Overall, how are you feeling? Those wounds were serious. I may have to reopen parts to make sure infection doesn't set in."

Jim was silent and puzzled. He let her do her nursing thing with a very cautious eye on her, Jewel and Briggs.

"Are you feeling of fever?"

Jim nodded his head yes.

She reached out felt his forehead.

"You could be hot from just being in this heat and the sunshine, but it looks to me like you could be starting a fever. Jewel, honey, hand me my bag."

Jewel brought the navy blue canvas bag over to her. It was a large bag, looked like it weighed a good twenty five pounds or so and it was about three quarter full.

Rusty reached in and grabbed a large bottle of liquid that was not labeled and a couple of white towels that were larger than bath towels.

"I'm sorry…what's your name?" she asked Stowe.

He just laid there in total confusion as to why this large surly busty woman pirate who the day before was fine with killing him, had quickly stitched him up on the boat and then the next day did not show the streak of meanness she possessed the day before. If this was a game that she was playing to keep him off guard, it was no doubt working.

"Jim…Jim Stowe."

He also couldn't believe that she knew all of this medical stuff.

"Well Jim, I'm Rusty. We got off on a brutal foot yesterday. But I make no apologies for being what I am."

Jim's perplexing body language was also present in Alan and Summer. He was like… "huh? What the hell is this?"

One could read the same statement from Summer and Alan.

"Jim, this is going to hurt. I can't change that. But, I need to do this to help with healing."

Rusty looked over at Alan.

"You may want to hold your friend. It will make him jump and squirm."

"That must be alcohol, then?" Alan assumed.

"Yes."

Alan and Summer both used their weight to hold Jim down in certain places. Briggs and Jewel just stood and watched.

Rusty probed the wounds with her fingertips. She didn't want to get the stitches wet, but then again, she really had no choice. Jim winced, moaned, groaned and jumped sporadically as she gingerly touched and moved sensitive flesh that surrounded her skill work in sewing skin.

"Yeah, this looks a little messy here…" she commented after Jim's sudden jump. "Yeah…this doesn't look right…"

She poured some alcohol from the bottle and Jim attempted to jump through the huge cumulus clouds that were hundreds of feet above them. Alan and Summer felt first hand how difficult it was to hold down a six foot five athletically thick man who squirmed and writhed in the ultimate pain. Both would feel the repercussions of that challenge for the next few days no doubt. His screams were loud and bold. His words were crystal clear. The quiet of the island afterwards meant that the villagers could hear enough of his screams to get their attention. No doubt all of the captives heard. Some turned to watch from the distance while some buried their head in their arms and cried.

As much as Rusty didn't want to repeat the process, she did. She knew she had to. And she knew she had to do the same for her husband, who was still sleeping back at their house.

Each process was just as bad as the first. By the time the fourth one was over, Jim passed out from the intense pain.

"Jewel, hand me my back again please."

Rusty reached in and grabbed two syringes and two bottles of liquid, again not labeled. Both bottles were different than the alcohol bottle. One at a time, she filled each syringe and stuck Jim. Alan and Summer were both horrified and curious as to what she was doing.

"What are you giving him?" Summer asked.

"First, I gave him something to help with the pain. It will make him rest, and that is what he needs. Second, I gave him penicillin for the infection."

Summer's puzzled look intensified.

"What if he's allergic to penicillin?" she questioned.

"Well, then we would have another problem to deal with..." Rusty replied. "But, this bag isn't a drug store, I am not a doctor. This is all you have. I hope he's not allergic, but if he doesn't get attention of *any* kind, he will die a more painful death than all the others."

"Then why not take him back to Paradise Key for real medical attention?" pushed Summer.

Jewel fielded that question with a show of strength. She grabbed Summer's arm and flung her around so she could look at her face to face.

"Because we are pirates. We live our lives the way we want to."

Summer was not amused by the arrogance shown.

"So you will chance his life because you are a pirate? What the hell statement is that?"

Jewel gave Summer a steely look and with a tone of intimidation and further arrogance, she said "that is our statement of life. And while you are here, you can choose to do one of two things...live by it..." as she took her fingertips and traced an imaginary line on Summer's facial cheeks "...or die..." as she turned those fingertips over and raked her nails firmly down her cheek to her throat.

Summer swallowed with a scared feel. Jewel's intimidation worked for the moment as she looked into the young pirate's eyes and feel the passion that gripped Jewel while she made her statement. Jewel then backed off slowly, letting her threat make its emphasis a bit longer.

Jewel then said matter of factly "Paradise Key is out. He will live or die right here. For your sakes, I hope he lives."

Summer felt a fire in her belly like she's never had. She wanted so badly to reach out, grab her hair and beat the piss out of Jewel. The only thing that stopped her was a look from Alan as they crossed eyes. Alan's look was an order to stand down. Summer shot back a look to Alan like she was ready to kill. Alan got the message.

Rusty scolded Jewel publicly.

"No need to talk like that Jewel. They are still figuring all of this out. We turned their lives upside down. You need to give them some room here."

Jewel looked at her mom cross and said nothing.

"Paradise Key is not an option. I will look after him later. If he develops anything, anything at all, get word to Briggs (she pointed at him), and he'll tell me immediately. I will come and do what I can. But I'm not trying to kill him, I'm doing what I can to heal him."

"Thank you" Alan said nodding and looking over at Summer at the same time. "We appreciate your efforts."

Summer got Alan's facial message.

"Yes, thank you" she echoed.

Rusty then turned serious abruptly.

"Okay, now to address your situation…" she started. "We will get your group together. We want names of everyone. First and foremost, before we say anything else, as long as the behavior is what it needs to be, we will all function well. But if anyone steps out of line, there will be punishment and it will be painful. You may be our prisoners, but we will open our lives up to you in some regards. And you have already seen what we have no problem doing. So, behave properly and life will go on. Don't and you will feel the wrath. Agreed?"

Alan looked over to Summer and then back over to Rusty.

"I don't think we're in a position to say otherwise. Agreed."

"Good" replied Rusty. "For what it's worth, your lives just improved from a moment ago."

"So what now?" Alan asked.

"Get a list of your friends together with names, addresses and such. As soon as I have that, I will speak to everyone and let them know what will happen from there."

"The sooner, the better I suppose" said Alan dryly.

Rusty reached in her bag and pulled out a notebook and pen.

"Here…write everything here" she replied. "I'm going to check on my husband, but I'll be back in about half an hour. If you're done, we'll proceed then. Briggs will stay for now and answer questions."

"Okay" nodded Summer.

"Jewel, you coming with me?" her mother suggested.

"I was thinking about staying here and observing."

"Okay. See you in a bit."

Rusty walked away toward the village. Alan looked over the notebook and pen and turned to Summer.

"Guess we best start now" he stated. "Do you know everyone?"

"No, I don't. You?" she answered.

"Nope. This will be a small challenge" he grinned slightly and dryly, his sarcasm showing.

Summer put her arm around Alan's shoulders.

"We'll make this work. I'm not sure how, but we will make this work. Just be strong for us."

Alan looked into Summer's eyes at first puzzled, then firm. He wasn't sure why she had suddenly turned inspirational and motivational, but he just rolled with it.

"We all need to be strong. I will help set the example."

Summer smiled and gave Alan a small but meaningful hug with her one arm, burying her face into his front shoulder.

"Good" she said muffled.

They walked over to where there was an old wooden picnic table that was beaten up from the weather. They sat down and opened the notebook. Alan started scribbling.

Meanwhile, Briggs and Jewel sent their attention throughout the area, scoping over the members of their group. Jewel noticed the younger ladies who were sitting in the sand next to the water. Small waves were buffeting the shore, at times spritzing the bare feet of Gianna and Eryan with a playful splash. The two girls were deep in conversation of some kind, but were out of earshot of Jewel. She wasn't sure why, but Jewel was insanely interested in what they were talking about. It was a strange turn of events for her, especially since she came off as a queen bitch moments earlier to Alan and Summer. Maybe it was the teenage still in her, although she was just a couple of weeks away from being twenty.

"Briggs, I'm headed over there" she said, pointing at Gianna and Eryan.

She walked slowly toward the girls on the beach, reaching them in a matter of a minute or two. She wasn't necessarily sneaking, but she was slow and quiet deliberately to hear what they might have been saying. They were talking about home and had no idea that Jewel was approaching from behind them.

Gianna became somewhat demonstrative in her movements as she spoke, and her body language caught Jewel out of the corner of her eye just standing there behind them.

She jump and shrieked like a huge spider had crawled up her leg. It scared the shit out of her, who in turn scared the shit out of Eryan, who also jumped.

"Hey! That's not funny! What the hell are you doing back there?" Eryan yelled.

Jewel had a hard time from keeping from laughing. The way the girls had jumped tickled her funny bone.

"Yeah…omg…like why?" reiterated Gianna.

Jewel stopped laughing after seeing how pissed off the girls were.

"Hey, hey…sorry. I guess that was wrong for coming over and listening, I didn't mean to scare you" she confessed.

Hmm…another side of Jewel had just been revealed.

"Mind if I sit with you?" she asked the pair.

"Sit with us? **With us?**" Gianna said. "Why?"

Eryan agreed and shrugged her shoulders…"yeah…why?"

"Promise not to say anything?" Jewel let on like she was suddenly one of them.

"Say anything? To who?" Gianna smirked. "You have us captured here."

Jewel looked down almost ashamed.

"Yeah, we do. Guess I'm sorry and feel bad, but I just need to chill with some real people my age. Will you let me?"

"Let you? Like we need to let you? You can just be here, it's your show here" Eryan said with noted hostility.

"Look, it's not the same. Yeah, I could come over and be a bitch and all, but that gets old. I need to chill…and I need to feel like I can do that. Being me is not all that cool…" she confessed again.

"Not that cool? I don't see it" Gianna remarked.

"Really…I'm not lying. You wanna know? Let me sit down with you and I'll tell you some things that will make you believe…"

Gianna looked over at Eryan. They crossed their looks for a good ten, maybe fifteen seconds while Jewel still stood to their left and a step or two behind. Finally, Gianna looked at Jewel.

"Okay, you can chill with us. I'm Gianna and this is Eryan…" she introduced.

"I am Jewel."

"Pretty name. Why did your parents name you that?" asked Gianna with sincerity.

"Actually, that's my nickname slash pirate name. It's because when I smile, I have two teeth that are filled with jewels. My real name is Starr."

"That's pretty too. Named after the stars I suppose?" asked Gianna with a grin.

"Uh…yeah…that's a true story. My parents say that I was conceived under the stars. So they named me after them."

The girls looked at each other, not really knowing where to go with the conversation. There was uneasiness in the air and an invisible barrier to break down.

"So what's it like here?" Eryan asked. "And what are we in for? I mean, are we gonna die here?"

"Well, nothing like throwing it out there, huh Eryan?" shouted Gianna.

Jewel giggled and smiled.

"You really want to know?" Jewel asked.

"Yeah" replied Eryan.

"Okay, what exactly do you want to know?"

"Are we gonna die?" Eryan quickly asked.

"Die? Well, anything is possible here, but I would hope not…" she responded as quickly as Eryan had asked.

"Anything is possible?" Gianna repeated.

"Well yeah, anything is possible" said Jewel. "Remember, we are pirates. We rape, pillage and plunder."

"Rape?" Gianna asked nervously.

"Okay…relax. Yes, we are pirates and some things we do are not gonna make you happy. But behave and don't be too vocal or rebellious and maybe nothing happens to you. If we become somewhat friends, I will try and protect you."

None of this initially made sense to Eryan and Gianna. These are pirates who just flipped their lives over into hell. They do all the horrible and frightening things that were ever talked about growing up. And after living up to the terrorizing reputation and image given to them while growing up just yesterday in the prolific killing of three and the sexual assault on Mandy during a take over, now the captain's daughter wants to befriend two survivors? That'll create a lot of head scratching when it gets around the camp, just as it was at that very moment to Gianna and Eryan.

Something fishy going on here in paradise…

Chapter 9

Meanwhile, back on the yacht which was still anchored just inside the tiny island's inlet, there was some stirring below deck. A small closet that had enough room for five bags had some movement. Following some jostling around for some air, the movement ceased momentarily, and then with a tremendous push of strength moved the bags enough to find a door handle.

She opened the door amidst just the noise of the ocean pounding against the side of the yacht.

Her eyes were glassy and the fog that surrounded her figuratively was thick and soupy. She didn't recognize her surroundings. The one thing she did recognize though was the knot on her head from falling backwards into the closet. Her head was still throbbing.

Once she managed to unbury herself of the heavy bags and leave the closet, she sat down in the dining area. Not knowing what to think, what had happened, where she was, and dealing with the disorientation that still affected her, she put her head into her hands and started crying. She could see the remnants of daylight though she had no clue the time or the day. All she knew was that the bright sunlight was only contributing to the physical agony she was experiencing.

She spent the next hour plus just sitting in that area crying.

Miles away in yet another direction of uncertainty, another awoke with a face full of sand in the grasp of a couple of sand crabs. Luckily, he wasn't in the grasp of any big claws ready to take a finger or toes off, it was just a deep discomfort that was felt. Spitting the sand out of his mouth and nose, he craned his head while still lying belly down in the shore.

"Where am I?" he thought to himself.

He struggled to move. His bearings were off totally. The only awareness that he could surmise was he that he was alive. All of the answers to all of his other quickly emerging questions were not within any grasp.

He felt incredible pain, but couldn't pinpoint an answer as to where it was, how it happened, and why he has it.

Moreover, he couldn't move much at all.

He had no idea where he was or why he just had awakened on a deserted miniscule island in the middle of what looked like nowhere. What he could see from his efforts to move his head and neck was pretty simple. Water and lots of it, surrounded him but for the small strip of land that he was attached to. No trees, no vegetation. Just a couple of sand crabs that befriended him…

It was as though he was stranded on a sandbar…still this was a much larger salty piece of land.

The conversation on the beach of the pirate island between Jewel, Gianna and Eryan became more intriguing as it continued on. It appeared that Jewel was not a happy pirate…but then again, what teenager is happy just before turning twenty?

"Okay, here's what you can expect from us…" Jewel started.

Gianna, somewhat smarter than the average jellyfish, wondered why in the world Jewel was opening up to them. The whole situation didn't make sense, at least not to her and Eryan. There was something weird about the whole thing…like it was being staged or something.

While Jewel went on with an explanation that wasn't capturing her attention, Gianna continued to try and piece things together to make some sense.

They were captured by modern day pirates while on a vacation rental yacht. They were captured by pirates that seemed to be stuck in the seventeen hundreds, meaning some very traditional pirates on a traditional pirate ship with old guns and swords and…well…traditional fashion.

"None of this makes any sense…" she concluded.

She interrupted Jewel in mid sentence: "This just doesn't seem right. Can I get a straight answer here?"

"Huh?" Eryan looked at her stunned by the outburst.

Jewel stopped her statements and gave her a surprised look as well.

Gianna reiterated: "Can you please tell me what the hell is going on here?"

A confused Jewel just looked at her.

"What do you mean?" she asked Gianna.

"I mean...*what the hell is going on here?*" she emphasized.

"You are on an uncharted island in the middle of nowhere..." Jewel began.

"Yes I know that, tell me something I don't already know..." attacked Gianna.

"Hey G...relax...breathe...don't lose it" Eryan said reaching out for her.

Gianna's reaction was not a positive one. Eryan embraced her to try and calm her down. She just lost control in the heat of wondering, simple as that.

Jewel wasn't sure what to say. In seeing how Gianna just reacted, her eyes teared up. She stood up.

"I better go. Please, if the two of you want to hang out, you're welcome to. Just have one of the guards come get me. I'm so sorry..." she said getting visibly upset as she turned and left in a quickened pace.

It was obvious to Eryan that Jewel was genuinely upset. That gesture of Jewel's made some impact on her.

Eryan calmed and consoled Gianna.

"What was *that* all about?"

"Sorry...I don't know. It just happened."

"Yeah, I'll say it did. Oh my God."

"I guess I upset her..." Gianna concluded, turning her heightened emotions into a smile.

"Yeah, you did just that" Eryan agreed.

"What do you think?" asked Gianna.

"I think there's some strange stuff inside that girl. It's almost like she needs to get some shit out of her system..." Eryan revealed.

"Yeah..." nodded Gianna.

"...some *deep* shit."

"Yeah..."

◀◉▶

Out of nowhere a buzz came from over the trees from behind the girls from the jungle area.

And as quick as that buzz approached, it went overhead to the right and quickly out of sight.

It was a seaplane.

Alan and Summer worked diligently to get everyone's name on that notebook page that was taken from the yacht to the island. They moved from person to person to ensure the accuracy of information and did so with a sense of urgency so they could move forward in their way of getting some semblance of what was going on.

That seemed to be the number one question on everyone's minds… not the why it is happened or what's happened or who are these peoples, but just what happens next. Everyone had pretty much accepted that they were just screwed big time. The thoughts are of what happens next as in 'let's get on with this'.

Names and addresses were listed in no particular order. At the bottom of the list, they added the deceased. Both Dyane Stowe and Mark Russell, two people who were not witnessed dead were still listed under the deceased. Alan thought it would be better that way so on the very slim off chance that either was alive, he didn't want to bring any undue attention to them and their situation. In other words, he didn't want the pirates to start an all out search of the yacht if Dyane was alive and still there. All in all, twenty two names were listed.

Upon completion, they walked the list over to the guard named R-Tard.

"I have the list for Rusty. Can you go and let her know?" asked Alan as he waved the notebook slightly in front of R-Tard.

R-Tard looked around, as if looking to find Rusty. He came up empty.

"Sure. Wen W-Wamon w-weeturns, I'll have him get hur…" he said with his unique way of speech.

With impeccable timing, Ramon was returning from wherever he was and R-Tard gave him the message. Ramon left immediately.

Then out of nowhere, shattering the peace came a scream…

"Dy-ane!"

Summer and Alan turned and looked over to where Jim was. He was partially sitting up with a ghastly look on his face. He was about fifty feet away and looked like he just saw a ghost. He screamed again.

"Dy-ane!"

They both went running to him. Summer took his hands and tried to calm him down. His breathing was rapid and erratic, his eyes sunken in and darkened around the outsides, yet all aglow like he was seeing something he had never seen before.

"Dy-ane!" he screamed out again.

Neither Summer or Alan could get his attention. Summer tried persuading him to lie back down, but he would have none of that. Jim was fixated on Dyane, but neither of his friends could figure out if he was calling to her because he finally realized that she was missing, or if he was seeing her in some spiritual way in front of him and he was reaching out to her in his own way.

His screams were half at the top of his lungs and then a more emotional type of pleading.

"Dy-ane!"

Alan thought this could be a last ditch effort by Jim before he gives out and passes. Summer scolded Alan for thinking that. In any event, they were both getting frantic as they waited for Rusty to return to their camp. Alan jumped over to R-Tard and got his attention immediately. He had heard Jim screaming.

"Hey, go run and get Rusty quick! Jim may be dying. QUICK! RUN!"

R-Tard stood there and looked around.

"What are you looking for? Get your ass in gear! RUN!"

Several of Jim's friends gathered quickly to see what the commotion was about. They all ran to where he and Summer were.

As R-Tard still hesitated with what Alan requested and the sudden chaos and movement of the group, Alan simply said "Fuck it" and ran past R-Tard and through a small opening of chicken wire toward the small village of about nine homes.

R-Tard just stood there going "Hey!"

Alan sprinted into the village and found the house of Bones and Rusty right away as Ramon was coming out of the door with Rusty. Both were appalled to see Alan running toward them. Ramon grabbed his gun and shot once in the air, then pointed it at Alan as he approached.

"Whoa! Hey don't shoot! Rusty come quick…I think Jim is dying…"

he cried as he held his hands straight up as he continued to get closer to them.

"Let me get my bag."

"Hurry!"

She was all of six seconds into her house, exiting with that life and death type of urgency. The three of them ran back to where Jim was, who was still in the same position. He was still calling out to Dyane as the trio arrived.

"Dy-ane!"

Rusty put her bag down and felt Jim's head right away.

"Yeah, he's burning up! Ramon, go get me some water…FAST!" she ordered.

He took off running.

"Everyone back off…give him some room for air…" she commanded.

She laid him down and then went filing through her bag. She grabbed a syringe and a bottle and gave him a shot.

"Come on Ramon…where is that water?" she questioned aloud. "We need this yesterday!"

Within seconds he was seen running back to them. He had what amounted to four bottles of water. Rusty grabbed one at a time and tried to guide the water into Jim's mouth and down his throat. Unfortunately for Jim, he began choking on the water and lost the contents of almost a full bottle right away. The second bottle was just as chaotic in trying to get him to swallow some. Fortunately, Rusty was more successful the second time around. The third and fourth bottles of water remained by Jim's side unopened and for a later time.

The plan was to have it handy to cover the next half hour or so, and to use it to gradually rehydrate him.

"He has fever. That's not good. Let's roll him on his side so I can take another close look at his gashes…" she said.

Summer stepped in and assisted Rusty in rolling him into a position where it was much more beneficial for Rusty to examine him. Just as she had done earlier, she poked and prodded throughout his wounds, looking at her stitch work and whether the skin was closing correctly. Obviously not in a sterile environment and with relatively primitive means and tools, Rusty did what she could to make him feel more comfortable.

She looked up at Alan and Summer periodically during the exam. The looks were not of a positive nature but of concern. Alan felt Jim's ship was sinking metaphorically.

Rusty finished the exam and signaled for the two of them to take a short walk with her.

"It's classic" she said.

"Classic? What's classic?" Alan questioned.

Summer took Alan by the forearm to focus his attention on her. He was mildly surprised by the move.

"Alan…Jim's infection, it's starting to spread. She means classic as in the infection is doing what it normally does. Am I right, Rusty?" she said looking for confirmation.

"Yes."

"Can't you do anything for him?" snapped Alan. "I mean, you have this huge bag of stuff here…"

"Alan, I'm trying, but what he needs we do not have here. He needs a sterile environment. He needs me or a doctor to reopen part of that and extract the infection. Then he needs meds and rest. It's a process and I don't have anything close to that process inside my bag."

"Then what do we do? Where do we find it?" snapped Alan again.

"What do we do? Continue to treat it the best that we can hear with what we have. Where do we find such a procedure? Probably Miami… maybe somewhere in the Keys, but for right now, he is here and not there."

"Look Rusty, with all due respect, I cannot sit here and watch my best friend die. We need to DO something!"

"I wish I could do more. Hmm…we could move him back to my house and at least make him as comfortable as possible. Bones is dying for some company…maybe they could help each other…at least spiritually."

"What about you or someone else going back to the mainland and getting the supplies that he needs to survive?" Alan boldly said to Rusty.

Rusty looked at him and sincerely gave it thought. She knew that Jim was entering the final flight path and that all he had was time. She knew what he needed, but at that time couldn't supply him with it.

"Is there anything we can do to help him?" Summer asked pointedly. "I know we are stuck in this mess with you (pointing at Rusty) but this is life and death, this isn't kidnapping and pillage and whatever else you are going to do with us. This is life and death. Haven't enough of us died already?"

Her emotional plea got through to Rusty, all the way to the heart. As

Summer's eyes filled with tears, Rusty's followed suit as well. But Rusty wouldn't give in to the notion of transporting him back to the mainland.

"It's too risky transporting him anywhere right now. We don't have the means" she said. "I can give him all the drugs that I have, but honestly, I'm not sure if any of them are strong enough to take care of that infection."

Alan looked away, shaking his head. The stress and pressure were overwhelming him. Thirty or so hours ago, he was leaving port with his best friend and twenty other close friends on a Caribbean adventure. Now, his friends are going down one by one…with quite probably his best friend in Jim Stowe succumbing next…

"Dy-ane!" Jim screamed.

"Dy-ane!" Jim whispered.

Chapter 10

B ack at the yacht following the tearfest, there finally was some movement as she stood from the table that was serving as her personal crying station. It was as if she could here the calls of her name in the ocean breezes. Her focus was becoming stronger as those breezes built to a near whistle coming through the doorways.

Feeling as though she was all alone on the ship, she grabbed for some confidence and cautiously began to walk around the lower deck. She was in search of anything that would help her realize where she was and what had happened. Her last memory was arriving at the boat docks with her husband to embark on this adventure that would reshape their lives.

Now, she had no idea what time it was or even what day it was. With the exception being the bright hot sunshine protruding throughout the yacht, she was clearly in the dark.

She moved from small cabin room to small cabin room, checking dressers, beds, and closets for any clues whatsoever. Maybe a cell phone was left behind. All she knew was that she couldn't find hers.

Dyane was engrossed in an eerie feeling. Once surrounded by twenty one others in sharing this ship, she was now all alone in the cabin areas with the sights of everyone's possessions, but no one around. It was as if they just vanished into thin air, leaving things just as they were, neat and untouched. At least that was the scene in almost all of the rooms.

The eating area was a completely different story.

Supplies of all kinds, food and dishes were strewn all over. It looked at though there were some mighty struggles there, but she couldn't recall anything happening there that she was a part of.

In one of the cabins she found a cell phone on a bed next to a gym bag full of summer clothes.

"Yay!" she whispered to herself in a mini celebration.

She picked up the phone and flipped it open.

"I wonder where Jim is...shall I call him?" she said playfully.

She tried dialing her husband's number. Nothing. She tried again. Same result. She looked at the phone frustrated. It wasn't even working.

"Damn...what the heck..." she said aloud.

She played with the phone, but came away still frustrated. The phone kept asking for a code to unlock the keypad.

"There's a code I have to put in? DAMN!" she whined. "What good are *you?*"

Dyane tossed the phone on the bed and semi-stormed out of the room. She walked about ten paces or so showing the signs of frustration, and then turned abruptly around and cruised back to her original spot. She picked up the phone again and reexamined it. Nothing had changed.

"Shit" she said. "Gotta find another."

She didn't want to look through bags for a couple of different reasons... privacy being first and foremost. She had no idea what was going on, so she actually had some inklings that everybody may return; just like they had gone on a group swim...or something. Dyane always had a good positive heart, so she always thought optimistically. This was so opposite of her husband Jim. Jim always found the challenge and struggle in everything and his sense of humor mirrored Alan Mayes in the sense that it was drier than a martini and stinging like a cold slap in the you know whats.

Dyane continued to look around the room, discovering nothing that would help her in her quest for clues and answers. She moved on to another room. She came across more bags, but the same results: no clues.

She repeated the process in another two rooms before she came across her and Jim's bags that were in a small cubby hole of a closet. She opened her bag but found nothing helpful.

She laughed "of course nothing useful...I packed it!"

She opened Jim's bag. Summer clothes and toiletries...the usual were found. No help.

"I really have to teach him to be more helpful to me..." she laughed again.

There she goes finding some laughter in the face of unknown adversity. Yet, that's usually how she dealt with everything...but how would she deal with Jim's current situation?

He was still lying in the same spot on the island and weakening by the minute as the pain and fever increased consistently.

Rusty and Summer hit an impasse as Alan became increasingly upset. For the usually calm and stoic Alan, that was a stretch. But he sensed that Jim was losing the fight for life and quickly. Alan wasn't ready to concede defeat.

Rusty packed up her bag of medical goodies.

"What are you doing?" Alan asked her.

"I have to check on my husband..." she replied.

"Your husband? What about Jim? He's dying!"

"My husband isn't doing well either" she said.

"But what about Jim?"

"What **about** Jim? We can see how he is. And it is not good. I can't do anything else here. I am not a miracle worker. I need to help save my husband."

"To hell with your husband!" screamed Alan. "This is my best friend! We need to save HIM!"

Alan was so pissed that he almost blew a gasket in his brain. Ramon took exception to his lack of temper control as R-Tard and Silly Willy came running over to them on alert with hands on swords.

"Look. See this bag? It's not a bag full of magic tricks. I have no miracles..." she ripped into him. "I am not a doctor. I can do some things, but not others."

"Save him" Alan demanded in a more respective tone. "Save him."

"I am not a god. I cannot make decisions on life and death..." she countered.

"I don't care if you are not a doctor. I don't care if you're not a god..." Alan answered. "I only want you to save his life. And out of all of us standing here, you appear to be the most qualified. So do it."

"What can I do? I am at a loss here. Even if I reopen his gashes and dig out the infection, there's no guarantee that it will help. And he's not in shape for any of that anyway."

"So you are saying certain death. No options here, just certain death."

"It looks that way" she conceded.

"Then give me your bag, stand aside, and you tell me what I need to do. You won't do it. At least I will try."

"What? That's insane! You have no idea what to do. Hell, I don't even know either!" Rusty exclaimed.

"Well, someone's gonna try. He may still die, but damn it, we have to do something!"

"I admire your passion and loyalty, but you are only going to put him into more pain and suffering. Do you really want to do that to your friend?"

The tug of war between an impassioned Alan and highly emotional Rusty continued to escalate. Alan grabbed for the bag.

Rusty held onto it, turning away.

Ramon interceded.

R-Tard put his sword onto the sternum of Alan, not breaking skin as yet.

Summer was standing behind and to the right of Rusty. When Rusty turned away from Alan, she turned toward Summer almost hitting her. Summer grabbed the bag and took three steps away from Rusty. Alan stepped backwards as well, away from R-Tard's long blade.

What that all accomplished, no one knew. It was an emotional play to illustrate a point. After all, Alan and Summer had no weapons, so it's not like taking the bag from Rusty suddenly meant that they were in control of the situation.

R-Tard made moves to close in on Summer...Ramon as well.

"Wait! Hold fast!" Rusty commanded. "Don't hurt anyone else. It's just a bag. They are both emotional over their friend."

Alan and Summer were still on their guard awaiting what was to happen next.

"I applaud your passion. But you don't seem to be getting the big picture here..." she calmly told Alan and Summer.

"You have to have something in here to help him" Summer commented. "You gave him something before."

"Yes...I have some penicillin...but that didn't help."

"Then what is the next option?"

"There is no next option."

"You said something like surgery?"

"I can't do that."

"Why?" Summer was on a roll.

"For one, I don't know how. Two, we don't have the tools. Three, we risk further infection. We're going over no new ground here. I told you this before."

"How far away are we from the mainland?"

"That's not an option."

"Why not?"

"I'm not gonna give up our lives, our history, and our future because your friend is dying. We are pirates and no matter how weak and emotional you try and make me, I'm not giving my way of life."

"Rusty, we're talking life and death. Your husband is at home in a similar condition. Are you going to watch him die?"

"No I wouldn't. However, he is not as bad."

Rusty hesitated in her words. The thought that Bones could very well be in the same shape crossed her mind. A chill went through her body.

"I...I need to check on him. Now, give me the bag. We can do this easy, or we can hurt you. Either way, I need the bag. I will check on my husband and then I will come back and check on your friend once more."

Alan and Summer knew that they had run out of options here. They played their cards, went with the passion play which bought them a little bit of time and some emotional weakness from Rusty, but in the end, they both knew that their was little more if anything that they could do.

Summer turned over the bag.

"You just did the smart thing" Rusty said. "I'll be back."

Ramon and Rusty immediately left to check on Bones while R-Tard backed down to his original guard position, leaving Summer and Alan with the feverish Jim.

The fishing expedition arrived back to the island and if a full net was any indication, it looked like they did quite well for themselves. Caleb and Dylan were on that exposition with the point being to catch enough fish to feed their group for the day. Needless to say, everyone was seriously hungry and getting to a point of malnourishment.

Upon making back to the camp, Caleb came right over to check on Jim. Dylan accompanied.

"How's he doing?" Caleb asked.

"Hanging in there...barely."

"Have they shown any kind of interest in Jim?" Caleb questioned Alan.

"Yeah, they have. But it looks bleak."

"Why's that?"

"She gave a lot of excuses, equipment, not trained for this, you name it."

"What about getting him outta here and to a real hospital?"

"Caleb, we are working with pirates here. Do you really think that they care about any of us? I'm surprised we have made it this far...really" Alan confided.

"How bad is he?"

"Feverish. Weak. And calling for Dyane. I don't think that he has much time left, but who am I to know?"

"Wow. We have to find a way off of here, not just for us, but for him especially."

"I'm all ears. You have something in mind?"

"Al, these are modern day pirates, right?" inquired Caleb.

"I would guess...what are you getting at?" Alan asked.

"Think about this...modern day pirates take us over and hold us captive...for what? What could we possibly have that would interest them?"

"Good point so far..." replied Alan.

"Now think about this...modern day pirates...right? This is 2011, right?"

"Yeah..."

"Well then riddle me this Batman, what are modern day pirates doing in a primitive wooden pirate ship chasing us down? Granted we were in a yacht, but a real lookalike pirate ship hunting us down? What's up with that?"

"Okay...I'm still following you Caleb...two good points. Where are we going with this?"

"Al, think about this...modern day pirates...traditional ship...doesn't make sense, right?"

"Right..."

"And what about those swords? What is truly up with that? When I was in the service and battled some of those Somalian pirates, hell, they had machine guns...and motor boats...shit that would blow these muthas away..."

"Yeah...I agree with all of your points Caleb, but what are you trying to say?"

"Al, there is no way on God's green earth that these guys are living back in the 1800's. Come on, how gullible do they think we are?"

Dylan agreed.

"Hey, we saw some stuff on their ship while fishing. Caleb is right. This makes no sense. They have to be hiding stuff…somewhere. There is no way that these are pirates and this is their way of life…" Dylan let on.

Caleb interrupted in agreement pushing the point further.

"There's no way that these people survive like this. If they are truly pirates, it's about drugs and running them, it about high stakes shit…big bucks and big whammies…"

"Okay…" Alan continued to agree.

"I'm telling you Alan, they are hiding some shit around here… they've got to be. I'm talking speed boats, high tech weapons, drugs, everything."

"Caleb, I understand you points and I agree. You have some thoughts on a plan? Can you get us out of here?"

"Dylan and I were working on it. Doesn't it seem odd that they don't tie us up? I mean, they gave Dylan and I a lot of freedom on the fishing trip. Yeah we worked our asses off, but if we wanted to jump, we could have. I have no idea if they would have left us out there or shot us or turned and run us over, but it did seem strange that we were able to do the things we did if we were slave like prisoners…"

"I've got to tell you guys, a lot of this makes no sense.,," Alan confessed. "I'm baffled."

"Me too" Summer nodded.

"Okay, so you know, we are thinking of somehow leaving camp and searching for their hidden toys. Dylan and I are convinced that they have some and that they are here…if we can find them and get all of us to them, we can make a break for the open seas and take our chances…" Caleb unveiled.

"I like your thinking" smiled Alan.

Chapter 11

The afternoon came and went quickly in the hot sun…judging by the angle of the sun, it must have been somewhere around six in the afternoon. There were four new guards looking after the full compliment of eighteen captives now. Alan and Summer had a much more new and cynical mindset to this whole experience thanks to Caleb and Dylan. Rusty returned to the compound with Ramon. Patients were running out.

"How's your friend?" she asked Alan.

"Do you care?" Alan smart mouthed at her.

"Wouldn't have asked if I didn't" she tartly replied.

"If you cared, you'd take him to the mainland for treatment" he said staunchly.

"We've been over this" she responded with irritation.

"Maybe we need to revisit this" Alan said dryly in a push of power.

She was not impressed.

"Maybe we just need to kill him and get it over with."

Alan hesitated not knowing how to respond. She took his play and one upped him.

"Maybe you do" he said in topping his adversary in aggression.

Summer and some of the surrounding captives could be heard giving out a hush. Alan was growing more aggravated and decidedly pushy.

Again, she was not impressed.

"And after I kill him, I need to kill you too…" she said in a stern medium tone voice.

"Well then…get it over with. I'm sick and tired of this bullshit. We're on vacation and you want to kill everyone. Why? Who the fuck knows?" screamed Alan as he lost his temper.

The blood running through Rusty's veins was boiling and she was ready to explode.

She grabbed Summer by her long curly tresses and brought her next to her. She held her by her throat as she took out a gun and put it in her right ear.

"Is that what you call leadership?" Rusty yelled.

Rusty cocked the gun and was ready to pull its trigger.

Summer was in shock. Again everyone surrounding the group exhaled a hush. Alan said absolutely nothing as Rusty held the loaded and cocked gun to Summer's head.

The next move was Rusty's.

Dyane continued her treasure hunt below deck on the yacht. There was water in a refrigerator there and some snacks that were unpacked before the takeover, so at least she had something to keep her going. The afternoon ended much like it had begun, going through rooms. As the sun slid through the sky, she became more aware and accepting that she was alone on the boat.

Following a water and Pop Tarts break, she cautiously headed up the stairs to the deck. She stopped after climbing just the third step. She saw all kinds of blood on a broken door frame and more blood all over the deck.

Chills ran through her as she was horrified by what her eyes were witnessing.

"Oh my God" she thought.

She doubled over and mouthed the name of her husband several times though she was totally left breathless. Her insides shook uncontrollably for a couple of instants.

She didn't realize it but there was a tremendous boat anchored right next to the yacht. It was behind the doorway where she was doubled over.

A couple of noises from there shattered her mindset and gathered her attention. She peeked behind the doorway and saw the massive pirate ship.

"Oh my God…make this a dream…make this a dream…" she said over and over to herself.

While she was being overwhelmed in the moment, two pirates came out from their ship and onto its deck. They were carrying boxes of supplies. Neither saw Dyane, even though she was standing a bit into the open for them to see.

She was frozen, scared and not knowing what to do.

The two pirates made some more sharp noises which appeared to snap her out of her trance. She scooted back into the doorway before they could see her.

But now she was left with infinite questions to ponder as she stood in the doorway out of sight…

First and foremost…What the heck is going on?

With little clues as to the answer to that question, a series of more questions flashed into her mind, all with the same answer as the first question. She had no idea.

Dyane allowed quite a bit of time to pass as she surveyed the area around her and became as comfortable in her surroundings as possible. She could reason some things, but found it nearly impossible to explain to herself what a mammoth pirate ship was doing anchored pretty darn close to the ship that she was standing on all alone.

One of her first cracks at an explanation was the thought of that was where all of her friends were, gathered for a party of some kind. But that got ruled out over time since there was really little to no noise coming from that ship and the sign of life was but two leathery, beer bellied, unattractive pirates doing what looked like chores of some kind.

Other than that ship, she was surrounded by water…and lots of it. The yacht was anchored a long ways from the island, just inside the inlet's outer boundary. Oddly enough, though in the water, it was well hidden by sporadically placed and growing trees…outgrowth from the bottom of the inlet. It was a very strange type of setting…but the trees roots were anywhere from eight to thirty feet below the water line. They were large above water and provided considerable shade and cover. What made it even more unusual was that they were growing in salt water. Anyone with a biological background in marine biology or agricultural forestry…or marine forestry if that is even a category… can figure out that large palm, palmetto, banana, umbrella or any other tree doesn't grow in salt water.

Ahhh…but is that true?

Those trees were real and not a figment of anyone's creative imagination, just like the actual pirate ship that was anchored behind the doorway that Dyane was analyzing in.

"This is way too freaky…" she whispered to herself.

As the time passed and she became more and more accepting of the fact that the pirate ship is for real, she turned her analytical skills over to the different blood stains that were scattered over a large area of the deck. She didn't know anything about what had happened. Heck, she had no memory at all about leaving the dock. So trying to piece together anything from all of the unknowns tied to the blood stains was doing nothing for her except scrambling her levels of sanity.

During the large amounts of time that passed with her analyzing, she would focus in and out on the blood. Most of the time that she did think about just the sight and thought of the blood churned her stomach to the point of lightheadedness and strong nauseousness. Yes, she was battling fatigue and hunger and thirst. Add to that the battles of the unknown and where her mind was taking her in order to come up with anything that could remotely explain this scene. But it was in her nature to find answers and understand everything that she encountered.

She examined the doorway over and over looking at the pieces that no longer were a part of it. She even wandered back below deck to try and piece together some of the things that were strewn about. The only times she snapped back to the current reality was when some of the noises the two pirates would make shattered her focus. That would always send chills up and down her spine.

At times she would even hear them speak and would try to listen. She needed clues. She needed information of any kind. While she thrived on challenges of mystery, the longer this one dragged on, the more impatient and frustrated she was becoming.

She moved closer to the side of the ship that was closest to them. Cautiously she tiptoed, sidestepped and crawled so as not to be seen. She bettered her position, no doubt, and she waited for anymore chattering from the two men.

Alas, it was not forthcoming.

Minutes later they both descended a rope ladder off the side of the ship and settled into the much smaller rowboat and off they went back to the island. Disappointed she watched them intently, following their direction and committing it to memory.

The sun was beginning to slide into the western frontier taking its light with it. Dyane was still settling herself on the yacht, being extra careful not to make any noises or sudden movements that would draw attention to her or the boat. But make no mistake, she was taking everything in and formulating just what she would do next. She knew that if there was any trouble that had happened with the others in her group, that that trouble would eventually come after and find her. So, she knew that she would need to be off of the yacht by tomorrow morning latest.

Meanwhile back on the island, there were some transitions to deal with as the sun set on their second day of vacation and their second day of captivity.

Rusty backed down after a terse standoff with Alan and Summer. She realized that the frustration was getting to both sides here, to Alan and his group as well as her and her pirates. With the gun to Summer's ear, Rusty regrouped, let her go and left immediately for her digs and where Bones, her husband, was in some sort of recovery mode from his injuries.

That left the vacationers all huddled together around Jim and Alan and so forth. They weren't about to waste any time. The guards had retreated back to their posts. So, a group of them helped move Jim into the building with the beds. It was hotter and stuffier in there, but the idea was that he would be able to sleep better in there as the temperature cooled off at night.

Everyone followed them into the building. It was tight quarters getting everyone inside there, but they did it without too much sacrifice.

Alan addressed the group.

"Okay, we are nearing the end of our second day of captivity...who wants to go home? Raise your hands..."

Everyone raised their hands.

"Okay, who wants to stay? Raise your hands..."

No one raised their hands. It was unanimous.

"Now that we are all in agreement, what will you do to get out of here?" posed Alan.

The group looked around with confused faces.

Alan reiterated.

"Gang, we are not going to be able to just walk out of here. We're going to have to do something risky and challenging and probably something downright dangerous…" he deadpanned in his usual dry wit and faceless expression.

Caleb jumped up to show some leadership skills.

"Al, Dylan and I have been talking about some things. We're looking for a way out, even though it doesn't look good right now. I believe this group of alleged pirates has some pretty big weaknesses. We are exploring what we could do about them. We need to know, before we overstep anyone, is that is everyone with us? We do not want to leave anyone behind. We live and die as a group. But we will not do anything if even one person is not committed to what we will try and do."

Everyone looked around at each other, some with blank stares and others looking to say something profound.

"Please, we need everyone's thoughts. Don't be afraid to speak. If you are scared to do anything, say so. We need to know these things before we waste time on escape plans and then find out someone doesn't want to do it…" said Caleb in a direct but hushed tone so the guards wouldn't hear him.

"Hey, I am not only scared but concerned that my fat ass can't really do anything risky and dangerous…" Kathleen pointed out to her husband.

Kathleen was a bit chunky from the waist down and didn't have a lot of confidence in her Arnold Schwarzenegger action star impersonation. A few others nodded their heads in agreement, not that Kathleen was overly heavy, but that they were concerned about trying to be action heroes.

"Okay, I see there are quite a few of you that are concerned. That's okay. We will take that into consideration…" admitted Caleb.

"Take that into consideration? What does that exactly mean? Like you will still do something dangerous and leave us behind? Or you will formulate your plans to make sure you take all of us along somehow…" questioned Kathleen. "After all, you said that no one will be left behind…"

"And no one will be" Alan cleared up. "Look, we will let everyone know what we're thinking. We will get off this island together. That includes Jim, too."

"Okay…good" Kathleen said.

"Anything you want to share with us now Alan?" asked Mandy.

Alan looked at Caleb and Dylan.

"Not yet. We are still talking about some things. But if anyone wants to join the talk about getting out of here, let Caleb or I know. We will need help from as many people as possible. What exactly for yet, we're not one hundred percent sure."

"Then what should we do now?" asked Elaine.

"Just be as normal as you can. Tomorrow will be our third day. As much as we don't like it, we should be settled into here. So be normal. Don't do anything stupid that will bring any type of pain or punishment. We all have suffered enough" replied Alan.

"Amen" said Elaine.

"Amen" the group followed.

"Let's all get some rest tonight. Hopefully by tomorrow night, things will be very different" Summer said.

The meeting ended and everyone bedded down for the night just as the last beams of sunlight were retiring as well...

Chapter 12

The night was way too quiet for any comfort level. The only noises heard was the quiet waves as they washed up along the shore and the insect life all abuzz with whatever they buzz about. There was a nice cool breeze blowing in from the southwest keeping everyone reasonably comfortable as they visited dreamland.

The sun arose much to the same quiet fanfare. Small red lines of fire sparked the morning sky as they looked as though they protruded out of the sun much like the vapor from behind a Navy jet in the morning sky. It was striking to those awake to witness it. Otherwise, it was the morning's best kept secret for those weary ones who rejected their return ticket from dreamland to reality and slept right through it.

Ramon and Silly Willy made their way into the enclosed building and awakened everyone about an hour after sunrise. For those awake and just lying there, it was no big thing. For those lying there sleeping still off to fantasyland, it was truly a rude awakening. And for those who weren't there to participate, nothing was missed.

What?

For those who **weren't there??**

Say again?

Who?

What?

Yeah.

Oh the cool darkness of the night. The mysteries that are born and nurtured.

Ramon and Silly Willy had no idea. They didn't count the numbers. They only yelled and screamed for everyone to get up.

"Need two men to fish" Ramon commanded. "Everyone else get in groups for water."

The captives looked around at each other. Who's gonna fish?

The previous day, Caleb and Dylan were the fishermen. Uh oh. Where are they?

Without making any fuss, the sixteen others looked around to each other for fishing volunteers. They didn't want their shock noticed by Ramon or Silly Willy.

Alan looked over at Sean the Cop from Annapolis, Maryland. He was big and strong and could easily handle what Caleb had done the previous day. No problem there.

Alan gave him the nod and he volunteered immediately. He had pretty much laid low throughout these first two days.

Alan then looked over toward Hunter James. Still feeling the effects of a bad concussion and shoulder, he shook his head no. Alan understood.

Alan turned toward Joe Mont, who was nursing some sword slices of his own. He smiled and agreed.

Before leaving, Joe and Sean met with Alan to ask about Caleb and Dylan, who were the two who were missing. By the way, the pirates still had no idea.

Alan just shrugged his shoulders and with his usual blank look on his simple featured face commented "I have absolutely no idea what's going on."

Sean gave him a 'yeah right' look in return.

"I swear. I have no idea."

Sean's look didn't change.

"Guys, be careful, please. We'll see you later…"

"Gotcha" said Sean as he walked away with Joe.

The group broke into groups of five as usual. Ramon led them to the water. He sensed something odd, but couldn't figure it out.

On the other hand, Alan realized what those two renegades had done, but he couldn't figure it out either. Why risk something like that…with no warning? It could set off a deadly manhunt or piss them off enough to kill the remaining folks.

Luckily, at the moment, no one knew.

But where did they go? What were they looking to achieve? How did they escape an enclosed area? And when did they do it?

So many questions all borne of the mysterious night.

In looking back, Caleb and Dylan thought it best not to let anyone know of their plans. Following their chat earlier with Alan and the group, they felt the immediacy of doing something was much more important than sitting around and waiting.

So they waited everybody out.

As the night calmed down to a slow nothing, their fellow captives fell asleep quickly. There was no tossing and turning, only a deep silent sleep after two very wearing days of vacation. So the two of them stayed up and together quietly as they watched the guards, one by one fall asleep in the quiet boredom of the compound.

So it was so easy it was scary.

Of course, they had no idea where they were going, although they did have a plan. Caleb was a strong believer that the pirates were hiding a stash of modern day pirate goodies somewhere around the island. He and Dylan were determined to find the treasure and help everyone escape. It was a great idea in its raw state, but could they improvise enough to actually pull it off? They knew and understood the risks. If caught, they could and probably would, die. But after talking about it for the past twenty four hours, their adrenaline and testosterone levels were so elevated that there was no way that either would back down.

So after the last of the four guards had fallen asleep, they made their move.

Upon leaving the building and their friends, they went directly to the entrance gate and once through there, they took flashlights from two of the guards. They quickly debated about taking guns, but chose not to since the risk was far greater of waking them up getting the guns than it was for two little flashlights.

They did not head for the village. Instead, they headed for the jungle with the idea of circling back around on the other side of the village. They figured if they were hiding any modern day toys that they would be close to the village and not on the other side of the island.

So they set off.

Through the thick brush they went, disturbing any kind of creepy crawly one could imagine. The terrain was mostly sandy, but the brush was thick in places, so thick that they felt like they couldn't get through. Was it all of the late night big and juicy tropical spiders out spinning their webs and awaiting dinner? At times, yes. But the growth of jungle was just as much to blame.

The trek was a slow one, which didn't faze them. They had to be quiet as not to stir anyone. Caleb led the walk ensuring that the brush and the branches that were moved for him didn't make any unnatural sounds in the dark.

The pirate camp was dark and sleepy, which surprised them just as much as some of their other observations that they brought up to Alan earlier that night.

"Just plain makes no sense" Dylan whispered when the observation of the pirate camp being dark was brought up.

"Exactly" Caleb nodded.

They continued their journey going in a semi circle around the pirate camp. It took more than two hours, but they finally reached the other side of the village.

They found nothing of interest.

In fact, they found nothing.

They walked almost right up to the side of one of the pirate houses on the far side of the village. They wandered the beach there as well and walked up alongside the coastline for what appeared to be at least a mile. They found nothing.

Both were disappointed and didn't want to return to camp empty handed. So they pressed on.

"I know something's got to be here" said an impassioned Caleb "I just *know* it."

"I'm not so sure" Dylan began to waffle. "We've been over a good part of this island."

"We will find something" pressed Caleb. "Believe it."

"I do."

Even after the groups were all led down to the natural spring that was a part of the inlet, no one recognized that the camp was two short. Everyone just went on about their business as if nothing was out of sorts. They returned to camp and had some fruit waiting for them to start their day.

Other than that, it appeared to have the makings of a very boring day in captive paradise.

Rusty did not make a showing to the campers during the morning hours. That led to some speculation by Alan and Summer.

"Really surprised that everything's been all quiet today…" Summer said.

"Yeah, it doesn't add up. I would have thought after yesterday's confrontations that she would have been down here early just to bust our ass" Alan replied.

"You think that maybe Bones is worse off than what she has led us to believe?" surmised Summer.

"Quite possibly."

"You know, from the get go I thought when Jim leveled him into the doorframe, I didn't think he was gonna get up."

"Yeah…I thought so too."

"And then when I saw that piece of wood stuck in his shoulder, I'm like 'he's really screwed now'. You know, I thought his issues were far greater than Jim's. His were wide gaping holes…those are unstitchable and a lot more prone to infections because they stay open longer."

"Yeah, I agree Summer."

"So I'm thinking, maybe he's much worse off and she needs to be there with her magic bag of tricks instead of here. Jim is seriously bad, but Bones may be worse."

"You may be right. Let's say I go find out."

Alan got up and walked over to R-Tard, who was the closest guard to them.

"Hey, where's Rusty today? It's not like her to ignore us" he said with a touch of emotional punch.

"W-wusty? S-s-she's wit B-b-b-bones…" answered R-Tard.

Alan tried not to laugh at the stutter. Usually a very classy guy, it just caught him strangely that R-Tard was even a pirate. Between his accent and his stutter, he figured some stronger more impatient pirate would have made him walk a plank by now. Alan was successful in keeping his composure.

"How is Captain Bones? I know he was hurt" Alan asked.

"He is huwrtin weally bad" R-Tard admitted. "I huwd dat he may die s-soon."

"Wow, no shit."

"Yeah. Jewel is dare too."

"Okay, thanks for the information. I hope he'll be alright."

"Yeah, me too" said R-Tard.

The afternoon slowly crept by. Hot and humid and nowhere to hide.

Thick salt air clinging to the skin. Oh, what a feeling. The captives were simply miserable.

There was still no sign of Rusty or Jewel. Fact was, there really wasn't much sign of life at all.

———————◄O►———————

Dylan and Caleb were still walking the island, appearing very lost, in the stingingly hot and humid sun. They still had not found any pirate toys of interest, like speed boats and machine guns. They were thirsty and miserable as well, but they still kept the faith.

Caleb was still leading the way when out of nowhere Dylan tripped on something. He fell flat on his face, partially in sand and partially in green thick brush.

"Whoops" he said from the ground. "What the hell was that?"

"What the hell was what?" Caleb asked in part humor. "Looks like you enjoyed your trip."

"Dude, what did I trip over?"

"I don't know…your feet maybe?"

Caleb quietly chuckled. Dylan was still prone on the ground.

"No, seriously dude, what did I trip over? It was seriously hard, like metal or something."

Caleb gave a half hearted look around Dylan's feet.

"I don't see anything but sand."

"I'm telling you Caleb, I stubbed my toes on something that isn't of this island" Dylan guaranteed.

"I'm telling you that I don't see anything there" Caleb sounded off more forceful.

Dylan eventually got up and hobbled and hopped for a bit around the area.

"There's something here. I will find it."

He continued to put his pressure on one foot as he searched for the obstacle that took him down. No luck. He sat on a nearby rock and took off his boat shoe and sock showing off an already swollen and discolored big toe.

"See this? Am I imagining this too?"

"Maybe if you had some real shoes the bushes wouldn't hurt your prissy feet so bad little boy…" Caleb whined playfully.

Dylan put his sock and shoe back on and hopped back about ten feet. He saw something and went for it.

"Holy Jesus!" he quietly exclaimed, looking over to Caleb. "What is this?"

"What is what?"

"What is this?"

Dylan dropped to his knees and moved away some sand and plant life. He uncovered something metallic in nature, which was black and possessing an unusual shape. It was only partially uncovered, it looked to be a large object and with all of the plantlife growing on it and around it, it looked as though it had been there for decades.

Caleb wandered in to take a closer look, leaning over the side of the object.

"What the..."

"Exactly" Dylan said.

Chapter 13

*I*t got to be close to sundown and still there was no sign of Caleb and Dylan, and also Rusty or Jewel. The camp collectively had a strange feeling wavering through it, something no one could put a finger on. It was a strong restlessness as well as a combination of settlement and boredom. The whole issue of this pirate adventure no longer had newness to it. It had lost its emotional edge. Three days into vacation and the group collectively had had enough.

Jim was still hanging on by a thread to his life. Just how Jim was doing it, no one knew. His was a situation that baffled the mind. Deep cuts, high fever, infection, dehydration all leading to his clinging to life. If there was a positive side to Jim's condition, he wasn't screaming for Dyane like he had at times through day two.

Alan had his moments. Huddled around Hunter James, who was finally starting to feel better after his concussion, and Summer through most of the day, he went from intense leader on how to get out of there to restless camper, like being a caged wild animal. Day three didn't see the usual stoic Alan presiding.

The women stayed in groups throughout. Since there was no pirate intervention throughout the day, it was truly a boring day for the ladies. The young ladies sat on the beach and complained about a shitty vacation. They got a lot of tanning in, but it wasn't the same as what they were accustomed to. They weren't in their bikinis or swimsuits, they were still in their original clothes from the first day…and those clothes were dirty, dingy, and getting to be pretty malodorous. After three days, showers were a much needed thing.

The older ladies were in another group and they also bitched about a shitty vacation, but not as strongly as the younger ladies. Their greatest source of complaining was now the fact that they had spent a day there doing absolutely nothing. Their current fate had been accepted; they wanted to proceed with whatever was going to happen next. Their next great source of chatter was brainstorming their way to escape. They all came up with creative and colorful ways of escaping, though none appeared to be realistic in any way.

Then again, was anything they have experienced thus far realistic? Maybe the violence…no definitely the violence.

Mandy could attest to that. Her original clothes were torn up pretty good when Bones decided to make her chest a squeeze toy.

Anyway, it seemed as though collectively through the camp, the heightened emotions of being on life and death danger red alert had subsided down to almost a life as usual kind of green alert.

Alan couldn't help but wonder where Dylan and Caleb were.

"I'm telling you Hunter, this has me worried now. What happened to Caleb and Dylan?"

"They're probably on the other side of the island enjoying margaritas" replied Hunter "where we should be…"

Hunter chuckled. Alan looked intense.

"Man, you've got to relax some" he told Alan. "You look like you're going to go volcano on us."

"I can't relax. This is ridiculous. Between Jim and all this shit around us, we have got to get out of here. I still can't believe that Scotty's gone."

"Man, I'm sorry. In all of this, we have forgotten about him. I'm so sorry…"

"Can you believe this? Can you believe *ANY* of this? I can't. It's like we left for a trip that went straight to hell. Three deaths…including my brother. Jim is ready to be number four. Don't even know about Dyane. That could be five. Man, inside I am just freaking out."

"Yeah, I can tell. Al, you still need to do whatever you can to relax some. You've got to be able to think straight. There's a way out. We just need to find it."

"Well, hopefully we can find Caleb and Dylan again and they will have that way" Alan hoped.

"Agreed" responded Hunter.

Back on the yacht, Dyane spent the afternoon still going through and re-going through everyone's things in hopes of finding a phone, or anything that would help her situation. She had thought about raising anchor and just taking off to look for help, but her lack of sailing skills squelched that pretty quickly. That didn't stop her from revisiting those types of thoughts though. Time was making her that much more restless as well. There were only so many times and ways one can go through a ship in search of help before starting to go nuts, and she was getting past that stage in a hurry.

She ventured back out on deck again and realized the pirate ship was actually gone. This was late afternoon. She hadn't ventured on deck all day as she was so tied up looking for needed treasure below deck. Dyane looked around for the ship in all directions, but it wasn't to be seen. So she proceeded to explore the deck area much more closely, this time getting past all of the blood stains.

It didn't take her long to find something she hoped would be useful.

It was another cell phone.

While looking it over, she smiled and said a brief prayer.

"Oh God, please make this work!"

She flipped it open and checked for battery.

It was still charged.

"Thank heavens!"

She started to dial…it looked to be working…she started to smile and almost get giddy…

But then…nothing.

Wait, who could she be dialing? Nine one one? In the ocean? On the island? Coast Guard? What's their number? Jim? Maybe Jim would have an answer…

She dialed Jim's number. She got nothing. No sound, no ringtone… nothing.

She looked around.

She looked at the phone.

She finally realized that there was no service out there…no reception at all.

"Shit!" she said.

Then it hit her. All ships have a radio. That's mandatory regulations in case of emergency.

"Why didn't you think of this before? Dyane, you're such a dumb ass!" she scolded herself.

So she went in search of.

She stayed on deck looking everywhere. She found another cell phone and repeated the same process as the earlier find. Still no signal from that one either.

So she went below deck looking for the ship's radio. She didn't remember seeing anything like it through her day plus of rampaging through every room and everyone's things.

"Damn! I should have listened when the guy took us on the tour of the boat! Dyane, when will you learn?" she scolded herself again.

While this was going on, Caleb and Dylan were going in for a closer look at the object that had tripped Dylan earlier. It was black in color and definitely metallic. It also looked to have the potential to be quite big and heavy.

Only a part of it was sticking out from the brush. Dylan moved quite a bit of sand from around it, uncovering more of a protruding arm or spike. They had no idea what it could be.

Their curiosity peaked as they continued to move some more sand, and then tried to pull out and move some of the thicket that was covering it as well.

"Now you believe me that I tripped on something solid?" Dylan played.

"Yeah, I guess I have to now. I don't think you put this here just before you tripped" Caleb answered sarcastically back.

"I don't know what it is, but I know it's pretty solid."

"Yep...just look at your toe" Caleb pointed out.

"What do you think?" asked Dylan.

"Well, it has an odd shape, that's for sure. I don't see any markings of any kind" Caleb noticed.

More sand was moved and jungle was ripped out showing off more of its size.

"Wow...never thought this would be *that* big" Dylan commented.

"Yup."

The two guys dug deeper into the sand for more clues. The further they dig, the more strange it looked, until Caleb said...

"Stop!"

"What?" Dylan asked.

"Stop! Stop the digging" demanded Caleb with an urgency.

"What? What's the matter? You know what this is?"

"Yeah, I think so."

"Okay, what?" Dylan pushed.

"I think this may be a mine."

"A mine?"

"Yes, A mine."

"As in land mine? Are we gonna blow up?" Dylan asked all concerned.

"No, not a land mine. It kind of looks like a sea mine" Caleb replied.

"Huh? A sea mine?"

"Yes."

"What's the difference?"

"You mean other than one is buried on land and one is usually in the sea?" Caleb said mockingly.

"Dude, no need to get smart. I have no clue. But if you think my question about the difference was stupid, here's another...what is a sea mine doing on the land, mostly buried under sand and heavy jungle shit?"

"Dylan, that is not a stupid question my friend. I have the same one at the top of my list. Then again, it may not be a mine."

"Then what can it be?"

"I have no idea. I'm gonna go with the sea mine theory. Usually land mines are buried and we'd be blown up by now. This looks like a really old mine."

"Then we should stop digging?"

"Yeah, for now. But I am curious as to finding any identification on it. I wonder how old it is and if it is still potent. If so, get the hell out of here..." he laughed with wide eyes.

Dylan moved some more earth from it trying to trace an outline to see how big it was.

"Well, it appears we can touch it without any issues" said Dylan with a grin.

"Well, you're just touching it in the right area. If it's an old contact mine used in the 40's, there are certain spots that are more sensitive than others. So be careful you don't touch something that looks unusual" he warned.

"Do you know much about this stuff?" asked Dylan.

"I know a little about mines but I am no expert. Mines were used back before you and I were ever thoughts to be. I tell you though, it is quite odd to find one here…if that's what this actually is…"

Caleb circled the object and leaned in to examine it more closely. He noticed that there were several arms that protruded from it, each extending approximately eight to twelve inches.

"Yep…looks like a mine all right…one of those bottom contact mines used on sea floors. It looks way too simplistic to be anything else."

"Really?"

"Well, that's what it looks like right now…" Caleb said, scratching his head. "But what I don't understand is if that is a bottom contact mine, what is it doing here?"

"What do you mean?"

"Those were used in Europe where submarines were used. The functions of those mines are to blow up subs that sit on the ocean floor. Well, we're on an island. What the hell is something that's used halfway around the world during World War II doing here buried in sand and jungle?"

"Holy crap."

"Umm…yeah. But I could be wrong. It could be something else…" he said.

"Like what?" Dylan asked.

"I don't know. If we dig more, we better be careful…that's all I'm saying. It does look like a weapon of some kind. I'm sure of that."

Both looked at each other. Neither wanted to make the first move to walk away or continue digging. The stalemate went about thirty seconds, then Dylan made the move.

"Screw it. We're here. We're screwed. Might as well have some fun…" he suggested as he uncovered more weapon.

"I'm with you brother. Just be careful…"

Within a half hour, the sweat was pouring off both of them, but each carried smiles as they uncovered some markings.

"Look at these hooks. This isn't a bottom contact mine…oh no…" recognized Caleb.

"Then what is it?" asked Dylan curiously.

"This looks like one of those moored mines…but the question still exists…what is it doing here?"

"Wait a sec. A moored mine…is that more dangerous?"

"Oh yes, it can be. I'm no Navy man, but I know some things. Moored mines are like four hundred and forty pounds and they pack over a hundred pounds of explosives if I remember right."

"Holy shit" declared Dylan.

"Yeah, those little hooks look like handles to attach them to buoys of some kind. Oh yeah, these are powerful."

Dylan possessed a more scared look on his face.

"Don't go weird on me. I'm just saying. These things sometimes have a shelf life, sometimes they don't. Even though this looks old, treat it like it's live."

"Oh I will. I ain't touching it no more" Dylan promised.

"I wonder if those pirates know it's here. And I wonder just how long it's been here. And I wonder if it's live, or if we can detonate it somehow to help us get out of here…" said Caleb looking into Dylan's eyes but staring through them.

"That's a lot of wondering" Dylan replied with a chuckle.

"Hey, this may be our way out of here."

"Cool with me. What's the plan?"

"Plan? I don't know. I wonder if we can find some sort of box or compartment on this thing that can answer some questions for us" Caleb said.

Just as Dylan was to comment, a seaplane approached from out of the north. It came sudden, like out of nowhere. It was low, like it was treetop flying with a purpose. It flew right over the heads of Caleb and Dylan and continued on. It was a one time thing. The plane was there and gone before either guy could react.

"You see that?" Dylan asked.

"Yes, of course I saw that" replied Caleb.

"What do you think?"

"I don't know what to think. I didn't see anything on the plane that indicated it was friend or foe. So I really don't know. But why would a plane be out here in the middle of nowhere treetop flying over a tiny island? I'm getting tired of all these questions. I really want some answers."

"Yeah, I feel you" Dylan agreed.

Caleb went back to examining the mine. He was slow and meticulous in looking for any clues that could help him figure this out. Dylan went back to moving some ground, also slowly and carefully.

Another fifteen minutes passed with a small finding.

"See this?" Caleb pointed out.

"Yeah."

"It's a sensor, looks like a magnetic one. Looks like it doesn't work anymore."

"Does that mean the mine is a dud?"

"Oh no. These mines usually have two or three different types of sensors. Now that we found one, we know what it looks like. I want to find the others. I still think there's a way of arming or disarming it..." Caleb said.

Five minutes later, they discovered more sensors. They looked like pressure sensors. Both stayed away from them.

With nightfall approaching, they had to make the decision whether to return to camp, if they could even find it, or continue to delve into the mysteries surrounding that mine. One thing was clear though, they still hadn't found a way to know if it was armed or not...

Chapter 14

The overnight proved to be pretty eventful, so much more than the day was in the village.

There was some sort of buzz from the village most of the night, as well as noises that sounded like motors mixed in for a sprinkling effect every so often. There was quite a bit of people movement going all kinds of places. In any event, there was a lot going on.

Heard were some barking commands from Rusty, so the island dwellers who hadn't seen her for all of the previous day knew she was present in all of her glory. Although her commands couldn't be understood from such a distance, one knew that she meant business.

Her daughter Jewel also could be heard through the nighttime air, at times just screaming back randomly at her mother, and at times appearing to be in a highly emotional argument of some kind. Again, exactly what those subjects were could not be deciphered from the camp inhabitants.

There were pirates stirring everywhere. It became obvious that there was some kind of alert or emergency going on throughout the pirate village, but Alan and his weary and impatient group couldn't figure it out. The buzz around camp with all of the movement and unusual noises was just that…everything seemed strange, so for a while they dismissed them.

The only things that were happening in the camp of captives were curiosity and planning. Whatever miracles that were being served up by Summer continued to string Jim along as he teetered along the cliffs of life. He was pretty much out of consciousness and not able to contribute anything toward the curiosity and planning adventures of the night. But he was still clinging to life and that was enough as far as the others were concerned.

The only thing holding back Alan and the others in their current plannings was the status of Dylan and Caleb. They left camp over a day ago and still there was no communication at all. Obviously, though, how could there be? It's not as though the island had a coconut telegraph…

The planning involved the whole group for once in a meeting type of forum in the little sleep quarters dwelling. It was a lot of what started as brainstorming and as the night wore on narrowed down to a couple of possible scenarios that the captives were willing to try. All were good swimmers they had noted, so an overnight mad dash to the water and a 'quiet' swim back to the boat were not ruled out. They thought swimming would be a better option if they were going to jailbreak because water sloshing up against large rowboats would make much more noise than individuals. Then again, part of that scenario dealt with just where they would enter the water. By trekking down the coast away from the village a bit, they would have to endure some more challenging rocky conditions, but they would have a bit of a shorter swim and of course whatever noise they would make would actually be further away from the village. But how would they create the jailbreak? That part of the plan received much debate with no definitive answers.

Another scenario had them breaking for the jungle and improvising from there, again thinking that they would be closer to a much shorter swim to their yacht. The obstacles with this plan were several, especially since the improvising part would be totally of the unknown. Yet, they figured that any plan had myriad of mysteries and unknowns and that each of them were in reasonably decent shape physically to attack whatever obstacles were encountered.

The third scenario was just a simple 'wait and see if Caleb and Dylan come back and with what info they have that would help us' kind of plan. There wasn't much debate there because that plan was totally one hundred percent in the dark. Other than Caleb and Dylan rejoining everyone of course, but any information they would have is still unknown at this point.

Not one person wanted to leave the two explorers of the group behind; still everyone felt a restless impatience about staying any longer than they positively had to. All had the itches to take off and run, and thank goodness, none were stupid enough to try and go it alone. The camp was still guarded by four pirates, each being changed out about every four hours or so.

Interestingly, no one still had seen Rusty or jewel or Briggs for the longest time. They had heard them screaming off in the distance, but that was the extent of it…until…

Somewhere about an hour before dawn after the village had quieted down a bit. There was an unexpected visitor to the sleep house where all of the captives had just retired and had fallen asleep.

Eryan and Gianna were sharing a bunk when both were disturbed by a third person joining them in their tiny quarters. Both were exhausted and neither felt like opening their eyes because they both figured subconsciously that it was the either that was crowding them. A couple of silent minutes passed on by. There was no movement from the girl's bunk after the initial huddling of bodies. In those two minutes, Gianna ended up being the one in the middle and eventually became uncomfortable feeling a body on both sides of her.

It wasn't until she heard whimpering and could feel the steady stream of moist tears that rained down onto her neck and shoulder that she came back to full consciousness. Gianna still didn't open her eyes, but she was now full aware that someone was behind her and in a state of crying.

The mysterious body shook with another whimper. Gianna was startled. Who could this be? Summer? Did Jim finally pass? If so, why wouldn't everyone be awakened? All these and many more questions raced through Gianna's mind.

She was afraid to move.

Then she felt a heavy arm come across her waist and onto her belly, pulling her closer to whoever was shedding the tears.

Gianna knew whoever that was was indeed very upset. Again, she initially dismissed it as Summer. Yet, she had never witnessed Summer get that upset and search for comfort and support like this person behind her. Though, in thinking it was Summer, Gianna moved her arm so she could run it parallel to the arm draped around her, and then she interlocked fingers to show support. She brought the arm in closer to her and hugged it.

In doing so, Gianna's support move turned to a face now up against the back of her neck. She could feel the breath, uncontrollable at times, on her neck at the hairline, causing goose bumps and chills throughout her body.

The bodies held each other in that pose for several minutes.

Then, in breaking the silence, Gianna heard the words whispered "I am so sorry…"

She opened her eyes looking straight ahead wide eyed. She saw Eryan, who was just as wide eyed looking at Gianna. That startled Gianna as well.

"Why the hell is Eryan staring at me?" she thought as her blood pressure increased quickly.

Evidently, the arm draping across Gianna had also disturbed Eryan from her sleep, however she couldn't make out who the arm belonged to.

They both just looked at each other making faces that neither could decipher. The room was darkened with just a hint of light, so seeing eyeballs were discernible, but not face making. The dark just made everything that much creepier.

No one moved.

Then the feminine voice whispered again.

"I am so sorry."

Gianna's skin crawled with the creepies. Goose bumps erupted again and the chill she felt up her spine leapt off her shoulders and found a home inside of Eryan.

Both looked at each other like "Holy shit!" The wide eyes full of terror gave that away easily.

Both now knew that it wasn't Summer. They both ruled out Mandy, who had been a complete mess since her newlywed husband Dylan had left with Caleb on their secret expedition over twenty four hours earlier.

Neither could see who was cuddling with Gianna.

"Please believe me. I am so sorry" was heard again.

Gianna had had enough. Totally spooked now, she didn't recognize the voice or the arm around her. So she finally moved, switching hands in keeping her fingers interlocked with whoever it was. With her now free right arm, she reached around and felt the outline of the female who was up against her and still at times uncontrollably shaken.

She felt the weight of the woman up against her. She had seemingly large hips and an ass that housed a bit of meat to it. That put another charge of fright into her because the woman behind her didn't resemble anyone that she knew. As she covered the curves of her legs, non sexually, the young unidentified woman again put her face into the neck of Gianna, burying it into her hair and softly caressing her neck with her cheeks. She was still damp with tears.

Somebody was having a breakdown and Gianna and Eryan had no idea who the heck it was!

Gianna continued to turn and try and face her. Again, she could sense the genuineness of this woman's feelings to the point where Gianna had tears in her eyes.

As Gianna turned, Eryan tried to get some peeks at the young woman but came up empty in the darkness. Her face was so buried into Gianna that Eryan couldn't make out anything. The frustration of being in terror was getting to Eryan.

Gianna finally flipped all the way around and faced the person who was almost begging for forgiveness.

Their eyes met for a split second. Then the woman started crying uncontrollably as she buried her face in a snuggle into Gianna's chest.

"Oh my God" Gianna whispered as she slightly turned her head facing up to try and communicate with Eryan.

Eryan rose up the upper half of her body and moved into a snuggling position with Gianna. It wasn't anything sexual with her, but done out of trying to hear Gianna.

"What?" she whispered to Gianna. "What?"

"O-m-G!" Gianna repeated in a bit of shock.

"What? What?" Eryan said again with a hint of impatience and urgency. "Who is it?"

"J-mmmph-we-mmph-ll" Gianna replied heavily muffled because her face was being smothered now by her.

"What? Who?"

"Jwwwwwwwmmmnphl."

"Who is that?"

Eryan sat halfway up, still in darkness. She wanted some answers and became increasingly frustrated that she wasn't getting any. In the cramped quarters where she was, she maneuvered to get on top of Gianna and pry the unknown woman from her. She wanted an identification and wasn't going to be denied.

"What? What are you doing?" Gianna awkwardly said to Eryan. "Get down."

"I want to know who this is" she said as she still tried to separate Gianna from the woman crying.

Other captives rustled around on their uncomfortable wooden slabs that were being used for beds.

109

"But you're hurting me Eryan…get down!" she exclaimed in a shrieky whisper.

Eryan got off of Gianna, and her can opener move to separate the two failed. Whoever was clinging to Gianna had quite a bit of strength to go along with a thick type of body.

Gianna knew Eryan was pissed and tried to console.

"Eryan, I told you who it is. Relax. I'm not sure what's wrong but it's something major."

"Who is it?" Eryan whispered back as the whimpering and sobbing became intense.

Gianna held onto her stronger as the sobbing increased and then let go into a more gentler position as she came up for air. It reached the point where Eryan thought Gianna was ignoring her, so she leaned over next to Gianna's ear.

"Will you please tell me who this is? You are killing me!" she whispered.

Gianna let go of the emotional woman and swatted at Eryan like she was a gnat or tropical mosquito. The swat missed her, yet still infuriated Eryan.

"What the fuck, girl" she said appalled.

Gianna turned toward Eryan as the woman resettled into the small chest area of Gianna still blubbering. She knew Eryan wanted answers and fast.

Gianna turned as far as she could go and started whispering.

"I told you this was Jewel."

"Jewel?"

"Yeah. Jewel."

"What the fuck?"

"I have no idea."

"You have no idea?"

"None."

"I don't understand."

"You think that I do? There's a pirate clinging to my chest like she's breastfeeding. All I know is that she's cried more tears in the past few minutes than I have cried in all my years."

And the crying continued, totally oblivious of the hush toned conversation that Eryan and Gianna were having.

Gianna continued to comfort her still not knowing what had happened to cause such a thing to happen. A pirate daughter racing to two same age captives for comfort? It surely was an unlikely twist to this strange vacation turned nightmare…

Nevertheless, with all of the nightmarish events occurring on Gianna's side of things, nothing could have prepared her for what Jewel was about to say. She unburied her face from Gianna's chest and wiped her cheeks with the shirt Gianna was wearing. Gianna noticed and disapproved, but said nothing to her knowing that this wasn't the best time in Jewel's life. She waited for Jewel's next move, praying that nothing bad was going to happen to any of them.

Jewel looked up at Gianna.

"I'm sorry…really sorry that all of this happened."

"I got that. What's the matter Jewel?" Gianna said in a hush.

"I know this has been nothing but a nightmare for all of you. I'm sorry."

"I got that, Jewel. You're sorry. What's going on?" pushed Gianna.

Eryan craned her head. She wanted to know through the initial shock that Jewel was even there in their wooden bed, let alone hanging onto Gianna with all of her emotional life.

"My father is dead."

Chapter 15

"What?" Gianna said, not believing what she had just heard. "My father is dead."

"Oh my God, I am so sorry" Gianna said sympathetically.

Eryan was more like: "Oh my God we are fucked now" though she kept her silence.

There was some more movement from the prisoners. Elaine James came over to the trio, setting her arms down and around Jewel in a motherly fashion.

"Honey, I am so sorry to hear that" she consoled.

Jewel just went on crying.

Elaine hugged her, giving her room to move.

Eryan was not quite buying the sympathy thing just yet. Family death or not, this girl's family was holding all of them captive and not only ruined their vacation that most spent months saving for and looking forward to, but also ruined their current lives.

With Elaine moving over to the girls, Hunter, Elaine's husband awoke and overheard. He moved over to where Alan was sleeping and nudged him.

"Have some info for you. I know why the past twenty four was like it was..." he baited quietly.

Rubbing the sleep, salt and probably the sand out of his eyes, Alan remarked wearily "Oh?"

"Yeah...you may want to clear the sleep out of your head for this one..."

Still rubbing what was now feeling like glass shards from his eyes; Alan perked up a little and replied "Oh? Why's that?"

"Why's that?" Hunter repeated.

"Yeah…why's that?" Alan again questioned.

"Bones is dead."

Alan woke up completely and sat up.

"What?" he said loudly.

"Ssshhh" Hunter said. "Calm down. His daughter is here."

"Huh? His daughter is **here?**" said a disbelieving Alan.

"Yeah."

"Why?"

"I have no idea. But she is crying all over Gianna and Eryan. Elaine is over there now, too."

"Wonder what happened" Alan said.

"Al, he's dead. He died."

"No shit, man. I got that. But I wonder how it all went down…" Alan replied as he got up from bed and motioned to and then moseyed with Hunter out of the building. "This changes things a bit…"

"I would imagine so…" Hunter agreed.

"Just not sure how though."

"Exactly. We could be outta here fast, or it could get uglier in a hurry."

"Yeah…we just need to figure this out" concluded Alan.

"But this explains a lot about what happened yesterday with all of the silence and then all of the commotion earlier tonight" added Hunter. "I think maybe, just maybe, he took some wrong turns and after a day of silence, the wife freaked and hustled him to the mainland or something. I could swear I heard motors during that commotion."

"You could be right…" nodded Alan. "Just wish we could get in touch with Caleb and Dylan. I wonder what the hell is going on with them…"

As Dylan and Caleb rested below the twinkling heavens, they also were considering their options. But for the overnight, they had agreed on sitting still close enough to their newfound mine to know where it was and yet far enough away that they wouldn't do anything stupid…like accidentally setting off one of the sensors.

They also heard a good part of the commotion coming from the village and answered some of their own questions about whether the pirates were truly a modern day group with expensive toys or a hobnobbing group of traditional wannabes.

Both of them not only got to hear the sounds of some modern day motors loud and quite clear, but also saw the two of the toys as what appeared as an emergency on a mission was taking place. They couldn't make out the entire hullabaloo, but they instinctually knew that something took top priority in a hurry.

They saw Rusty, and heard her barking instructions. They also witnessed someone else that commanded everyone's attention, someone that was smaller in physical stature than Bones, yet had a much more intimidating way about him, if one could believe that. Neither Caleb nor Dylan could figure out this guy's relationship to all the other pirates, but both assumed that he was the number two or three guy in the hierarchy. This guy was a much sharper presence than Briggs, whom everyone had thought was Bones' number two guy.

Caleb could swear that his name was Katmandu. Dylan wasn't as sure. But Rusty had barked out his name a couple of times as the ruckus evolved with urgency.

In what they had witnessed, there were several pirates moving objects, one of which appeared to be a body. Rusty accompanied them and this Katmandu character led the emergency voyage. The vessel that was used was a high powered speed boat that was pretty large in size. It took all of about three minutes to board and get settled before they all sped off and disappeared.

After they became a small blinking speck on the horizon in the dark, the village was still abuzz. Again, neither Caleb nor Dylan could make anything out.

An undetermined amount of time had passed with Caleb and Dylan just chilling under God's lanterns. Since there were no discernible time pieces on the island, no one really knew the theory of time passage. So consider that it was hours later and still during the darkest part of the overnight.

The boat returned.

It wasn't the same boat that had left hours before.

No doubt there was something missing.

Caleb and Dylan watched curiously, noting the huge drain of aura that had enveloped the traveling team at the onset. Once again, they figured something was going on, and realized that whatever it was it did not turn out for the best, but couldn't determine exactly what that was.

As they rested digesting what had happened, there were noises that broached their area of silence. Those noises weren't the tropical breezes blowing lazily through the trees. Oh, no. They weren't noises associated with a passing shower that hit those same trees creating a set of sounds that were different some hours earlier just after sundown. But they were noises that caught the attention of military trained Caleb.

He stood up at attention and scoped the darkened area. What little juice was left in the flashlights were shone around the area, but yielded no answers.

The noises stopped.

Then there were noises from behind the duo.

Both about snapped their necks in looking behind. But again, they saw nothing but jungle. Their 'frightened meters' skyrocketed with the sporadic noises of movements that were emanating from all around them. The ironic thing was that these types of noises were now echoing around them because the constant buzz from the village had died down. Lord only knows how long those creepy little sounds were clicking off. Caleb was handling them best with his former training of Special Forces. Dylan was quickly becoming a nervous wreck. After more than twenty four hours on this expedition at heightened awareness, he was beginning to crack.

The noises left and reappeared several more times in a fifteen minute span that took over two hours of their lives to live. The guys didn't think it was an animal, and shrugged off an insect theory. Originally thought as a wandering pirate search team, even that theory was eventually shot down because the noises weren't consistent enough to give credence to.

And then, as if this person just fell out of a tree, there the person was.

"Holy shit!" exclaimed Dylan.

Dylan jumped so high it looked as though he actually came out of his skin.

"My God, where the hell did you come from?" Caleb pronounced more calmly.

"EEEEEEEEEEEKK!"

At first, neither Dylan nor Caleb recognized the person next to them. It was a darkened diminutive silhouette. They assumed it was female since the physical stature appeared smaller than both of them.

It was.

She was just as shocked as the two men, letting out quite a scream when she almost literally walked into them.

"SSHHH" Caleb demanded as he tried to put his hand over her mouth.

The darkness kept him from success.

She recognized the voice of Caleb immediately.

"Caleb!"

"Yeah...who are you? Identify yourself..."

She answered instinctually without thinking.

"Caleb...it's me..."

"Me? Me who?"

"Caleb...it's me...Dyane" she reassured.

"Dyane? Dyane who?"

Her voice did not register with Caleb.

"Dyane Stowe.,..Jesus, Caleb" she deadpanned. "I'm missing for how long and this is the greeting I get?"

Dylan was busy trying to fit himself back into his skin.

"Dyane, where have you been? God, we thought you were dead days ago..."

"Well thanks, Caleb. But I can assure you that I am here standing next to you two and not a figment of your imagination. Where have I been? Got an hour for a story?"

"Realistically probably not" he said dryly in his usual tone and pace. "But I don't think we're moving anywhere anytime soon."

"No? Why not? I have been moving all night" she quipped.

"Two reasons...one, we have no juice left in our flashlights. Two, we are standing about ten feet from a mine."

"A mine?" she questioned.

"Yeah, a mine..." he repeated.

"No shit. Like a bomb kind of mine?" she asked in disbelief.

"Yeah, a real mine."

"Boy this whole vacation just gets better by the minute..." she commented sarcastically.

"Trust me, you don't know the half of it" said Caleb.

"The half of it?? I don't know *ANY* of it!" she confessed openly. "I have no idea what's going on, where I am and why I am here..."

"I can understand."

"So, not to sound like a smart ass" she said in the dark "but can you possibly shed some light on what the hell is going on?"

"What do you know as of now?" asked Caleb.

"Assume nothing, because I have no idea about anything since we left Paradise Key."

"Seriously?"

"Yeah…seriously."

"Okay…better sit down…"

Dyane sat on the ground right where she was. She was totally uncomfortable and stood right back up.

The guys understood. In what little light was available, the threesome shared what was going on from each other's perspective. Well, two of them did. Dyane instantly started crying. Dylan stayed conspicuously quiet. Caleb tried to keep her as calm as possible so she wouldn't give away their position in the area. In doing so, he sheltered her from much of what happened.

That didn't slow her tears. It just diverted her focus away from her husband, who was still clinging to some specs of life, to the twenty friends who were also involved in the takeover and kidnapping. She had no idea the real extent of what had happened.

Her thoughts became rapid fire spoken thoughts and questions from herself. Her breathing became rapid as well, and the intensity of her body language and her spoken thoughts made Caleb reach out and grab hold of her.

It surprised her.

But it snapped her non stop behavior patterns.

She then felt a strange wicked feeling come up from her lower bowels that took off through her body, shaking her spastically for a good five or six seconds. The look on her face could be barely made out, but it was evident to Caleb that through her woman's intuition, she was needed somewhere else and in a hurry.

"Where's the village?" she asked on a mission.

"The village? Shit, we don't remember. We've been out her over a day…" She changed her look from urgency to fire.

"Caleb, don't fuck with me. Where's the village?"

Caleb felt the heat.

"I think it's that way, but…" he said, pointing behind Dylan.

She took off into the darkness suddenly, darting from the position she had standing next to Caleb and Dylan.

"But…that's the village! We're in the camp over in *that* direction" he half yelled in the empty air that once possessed her nearby, pointing in the opposite direction.

Of course she didn't hear him. She was already gone. She had no light or anything to protect her, and that worried the two men. The jungle was pretty thick with no real paths carved into it.

But she took off like a jack rabbit. She really had no clues just how bad her husband's condition was in the prisoner's camp. Again, call it a woman's intuition. Those feelings that she had emanated from lower than the pit of her stomach and shook her like a firm moist Arctic breeze caught her stark and raw right to the bone.

She raced.

It was in her mind that she had little time to see Jim again.

She hauled ass.

And through at least the beginning part of the journey for her, someone up above was watching...and watching closely. Any time that she was close to decapitating herself with a tree branch or tripping over a shrubbery and brush, those obstacles seemed to magically disappear.

Dyane left Caleb and Dylan standing there not knowing what to do. Do they leave the mine that they had found and follow her? What if the mine disappears? What if they all get lost? What if they get captured? What if...what if?

"Screw all the what ifs..." Dylan said. "Are we going after her in the dark or are we staying here until light?"

"Hate to let her leave like that, but she's gone. We will never find her in the dark..." replied Caleb.

"Shit, we should have never let her go..."

"Dude, we didn't *let* her go. She darted like a bat out of hell...totally possessed. She was gone before it registered in my mind" admitted Caleb.

"Great. Now what?" asked Dylan.

"I don't know, man. I'd rather stay here and be safe. First, she could run into a mine and blow herself up. Two, she could run right into a tree and kill herself. Three, she could run right into pirates. You don't think they'd like that, do you?"

"I see what you mean" Dylan said shaking his head. "I can't believe she just took off."

"Yeah, me too...and in the wrong direction."

The two of them settled down again, close to the mine they found and under the heavenly stars. They did wait until dawn to make a move.

Meanwhile, with her sense of urgency beating harder and stronger with each passing minute, Dyane continued to bolt through the jungle. Her luck began to run out as she drew nearer the village.

She was felled by a hidden piece of tree sticking out. It wasn't really a branch, but a thick trunk of growth with dozens of branches expanding its shape.

WHUMP!

Down she went seeing more stars than the ones that were lighting her way through the darkness. Of course, the direct hit caught her by surprise.

But being the trooper on a mission, she scrambled up to her feet and ambitiously shook out some of the venom from that sting. Her head hurt, but her insides were hurting much more with each second going by without Jim by her side.

Three steps after gaining her feet, she tripped over a hard thick root.

"Damn…did that hurt!" she snapped at herself.

That trip down to earth ripped both of her knees open when they hit flush against the staunchly, petrified soil.

She regained her feet, with both knees bleeding warmly down her legs. She continued to scamper as best as she could and within a short time she came across some signs of life and the pirate village.

There were only a couple of pirates standing guard at the village, but there still was some buzz in the heavy overnight air that made dark its darkest just prior to dawn.

Dyane slowed her pace to a caution. She was hurting physically from the run and falls, but the desires mentally of her husband kept her in motion.

"Gotta find him" she kept saying to herself over and over.

"Gotta find him…"

"Gotta find him…"

She stayed along the outside boundaries of the pirate town. She couldn't tell if she was in the right place or not, or even if she was any closer to her ailing husband.

While slowly scoping out the area and investigating the sights and sounds that she came across, she witnessed a couple of people returning on a motorized speedboat. The aura that surrounded them was somber, yet volatile. Within a few seconds of the docking there were yells and screams from the pirate Rusty could be heard calling Katmandu.

Those screams were not screams of joy by any means.

Katmandu wanted revenge for the death of his brother, Blackeye Bones, the Captain of this Pirate population. While Dyane couldn't make out all of the thoughts that were being screamed, she could tell that it was one of her group's personnel that dealt Bones his dying blow.

That whole incident frightened her to no end. Someone was going to pay for the Captain's passing and she found herself saying numerous prayers that he wasn't screaming about Jim.

That fed her desires to get to him even stronger. So she kept moving. She wasn't sure the direction of where Jim was, but she held tight to the line of direction she was on to begin with.

She bought herself a little time as Rusty had persuaded and escorted Katmandu into her house. From there the voices could still be heard, echoing over the breezes coming off of the Caribbean Sea that rustled countless trees. She couldn't make out anything that they were saying, but she wasn't going to hang around and attempt to decipher their words when they became clearer. She wanted Jim, so she kept moving…and moving… and moving…

Chapter 16

It seemed like the footrace was on. Though Dyane really wasn't aware of exactly who this character named Katmandu was after. All she knew was that this guy was pissed…mightily.

She stayed around the perimeter of the pirate village as she walked away from the part of the coast that housed the speed boats. It brought her back into the jungle a small ways, but once she had her bearings with the light from the village aiding her, she read the direction off of the body language and movements of Katmandu and was on her way.

Dawn was very much on the horizon. It was going to be a deep red sky.

Dyane took note of it.

"Hope the sailor's adage doesn't ring true today…" she said to herself under her breath in reference to "Red sky at night, sailors delight…red sky in morning, sailors take warning…"

Rusty and Briggs came fleeing out of Katmandu's dwelling a fraction of a moment after he did. With him flailing his arms and screaming about Bones and killing, Rusty and Briggs went into damage control and attempted to delay Katmandu on his hostile next moves. They caught up to him and were able to gain his attention about a quarter of the way to the prisoner camp.

"Kat, this will solve nothing right now…" Rusty was heard screaming at him.

"The hell it won't. Fucker killed Bones. Enough said" replied Katmandu.

"No, no, no…you have it all wrong" pleaded Rusty. "You weren't there…"

"I don't care what Bones did. He's a pirate. He does anything that he wants. Look…I'm a pirate. You're a pirate. What the fuck's your problem? Why are you protecting them?" Katmandu yelled.

"We have killed already. They are innocent people. They have done nothing to us. We have screwed their lives forever. They have nothing that we can want or use. What's the point?" Rusty continued pleading.

"What's the point? What's the point?" he argued back alternating looks between Rusty and Briggs.

Briggs shrugged his shoulders.

"We are PIRATES! Since when did we need any points?? Rusty you KNOW that! When did you get all soft? I know my brother didn't do this to you!" he screamed.

"Leave him out of this Kat! He gave his life, our life, being a pirate. Now he's gone! NOW HE'S GONE!" she cried heading into hysteria. "And, now for what?"

The dramatic scene unfolding pretty much in front of Dyane was touching, yes, but she didn't stick around to see how it was going to end. She noticed the direction they were all going in and saw the camp in the distance. She carefully continued in that direction, leaving the three of them to finish their scene behind her. With all of the screaming and hysterics, the noises that Dyane were making as she traveled were not heard at all.

She could still hear them screaming at each other as she approached the enclosed camp.

Dyane noticed the pirates who were guarding the entrances to the area and paused to analyze.

As the yelling became even more intense behind her, she noted the guards were giving their full attention to it. As they chatted back and forth not really knowing what the arguing was about, they moved from their position aimlessly.

The whole camp was abuzz now with the noise created by Katmandu, Rusty and Briggs, who had entered into the verbal assaults. Dyane noticed that a couple of her friends on the yacht, Elaine and Karen, were outside the building where everyone was sleeping. The yelling had got their attention as well. They were up close to the fence, yet still about fifty feet or so from the guards.

Also outside but close to the building were Alan and Hunter, deep in conversation about what options were current and making plans. Inside the building that no one knew about was Jewel, Rusty's daughter, who was snuggled up next to Gianna, looking for some comfort to what had just happened to her father, Bones.

Dyane took a second to feel a swelling of warmth come over her. The feeling was overwhelming to finally believe that she will be reunited with her friends, and ultimately her husband Jim. But a second was all that she had as the scene continued to intensify.

Katmandu, Rusty and Briggs were on the move heading toward the camp of captives. Whatever was said wasn't getting through to Rusty. She was still pleading, loud and clear, through hysterical screams and whines. And she was now tugging on Katmandu, trying to keep him from the captives.

As Katmandu approached, the guards went towards him to meet up with him, leaving the front entrance open and unguarded. With all of the emotional chaos diverting any attention from the camp entrance, Dyane knew it was now or never to make her move and reunite.

Waiting never entered her mind.

Hesitation was no longer in her vocabulary.

In an all out sprint from the cover of jungle and into the dawning of daylight, she went for the opening…

…no doubt the longest twenty seconds of her life…

…it just went on…

…and on…

…as the screaming and chaos continued to build…

…it was deafening…

…and she heard nothing…

…as she focused on the opening…

…the longest twenty seconds of her life…

…hoping that no one would notice her as she sprinted into the open…

…almost there…

…not looking back…

…out of breath running in the sand…

…gotta get there…

…so…

…so…

…close…

Chapter 17

$\mathcal{M}$ ark awoke with the dawn for the first time in two days. He was still lying on the beach of some incredibly small island that could probably qualify as an overgrown sandbar in the middle of nowhere. His eyes opened for the first time dry and painful. Going to rub the discomfort out of them, he raised his hands only to breach them with lots of sand. The feeling of glass shards were everywhere as he screamed. So was the pain.

"Owwwwwwwwwwwwww" he screamed.

The pain wasn't only from his eyes. He was still lying in almost the same position as he was when he first awoke days earlier from his exciting escape swim and shooting from the original pirate take over. It was the scene made for movies, no doubt, and he actually survived such a climatic episode…well at least til now.

His pain was all over his body. And it was that pain that probably knocked him back out for the two days he lay there after originally becoming conscious after his fleeting swim.

He had trouble moving. He had issues thinking. And well, although now awake once again, he truly wished at the moment that he wasn't.

Slowly he moved each limb. If his muscles weren't all knotted up, then it was the extreme sunburn he had on his exposed skin that got him. But at least he was beginning to function once more, and even though his head wasn't necessarily in it, his heart was all about being alive.

Just as slowly as he physically recuperated, the memory of what happened on the boat reappeared. He analyzed what happened as he moved his weary beaten up body into the water, using the warmth of the sea therapeutically to energize his muscles. Stretching each limb cautiously wary of spasms, he thought about the events that led to his current standing.

Were there really pirates?

Did he actually make those moves on the yacht?

Did he really kill Ratface?

And did he swim unmolested by sharks and barracudas to this tiny island of sand?

Or, was this all just a nightmare?

He looked down at the blood trails on his clothes.

"Nope...no nightmare...this is reality."

He snickered, and then winced with some pain as the water washed into his injuries.

"Shit."

Dyane made it uncontested through the opening of the fence to the captive's compound. How she accomplished that, she didn't know. But with all of the commotion still almost one hundred feet away from the entrance, it could be understandable. It wasn't as if she was sneaking around in the dark. Dawn had come and her body could have easily been made out.

She ran right to the doorway of the sleeping quarters. Dyane didn't bother to stop by or signal Elaine or Karen who were further into the camp along the fence. Both of them were taken up by the excitement created between Rusty, Katmandu, Briggs and the guards.

She also didn't go towards Alan and Hunter who had moved in a different direction outside the hut. In her mind, it was all about getting out of anyone's possible sight...and finding the sight of her husband Jim.

As she entered the large room with the beds, she was almost completely out of breath. She doubled over with hands on both knees to try and catch her breath, but that didn't work. She raised her head to see if anyone was awake and about, but she didn't come across anyone recognizable immediately. The light in the quarters was minimal, and most people were nothing more than sleeping or snoring lumps on their wooden slabs.

She took both her arms and reached for the sky as her breathing was still heavy and mostly out of control. Reaching up with arms over head was helping to open her lungs up, but more importantly, it gave her some stable sightlines as she walked around the room looking for her husband.

Dyane walked right by the bed being shared by Gianna, Eryan and Jewel and witnessed the hushed whimpering by Jewel, though did not stop to investigate. All three were still silhouettes in the somewhat darkened room. She continued to slowly walk.

"Jim...Jim" she called out in a whisper.

Other than the whimpering, she heard nothing.

"Jim...Jim" she repeated as she continued her tour around the room.

Still nothing was heard. There was no movement in the beds.

Without warning, Elaine and Karen bolted into the room.

"Oh my God, they're coming!" shrieked Karen.

Both women just about walked straight into Dyane.

They looked at each other with squinted eyes in a shocking stare for a few frozen seconds.

"Oh my God...Dyane?" Elaine queried.

"Dyane?" Karen echoed.

Before Dyane could answer, both women hugged her.

The hug was short lived.

"They're coming" Elaine said.

Yes, the commotion continued outside and it was getting closer.

"Where's Jim?" was all Dyane could muster.

"Jim? He's over here" Elaine replied.

Jim had a bed all to him and was struggling to breathe.

"What's wrong with him?" Dyane asked as she look on in horror.

She grabbed a hold of his hand.

"What happened to my Jim?"

"You don't know?" answered Karen.

"No."

"Oh..." Karen said with much sorrow.

Dyane's look went towards going hysterical.

"Oh my God, from what I can see...what's wrong with him? What happened? Please tell me!"

Elaine and Karen looked at each other. Elaine took the lead.

"Jim responded to the takeover on the boat by going after their captain. He sexually assaulted Mandy and was laughing about it when he raced into him with his shoulder."

"What?" Dyane shrieked in disbelief.

"Well, before that he was sliced pretty good by the sword, remember Elaine?" contributed Karen.

"Yeah, that's right. And then he got cut up some more by another sword. The gashes are deep" said Elaine.

"Oh my God" replied Dyane as she put both hands over her cheeks and open mouth. "Oh my God…Jim…"

"Summer has been watching over him with Alan. Those two can give you a more detailed accounting of the facts as well as his current condition…" Elaine continued.

Dyane started crying. The tears increased quickly.

"All we know is that he is in really bad shape" finished Elaine.

Through the tears, Dyane asked "How bad?"

"From what we know…" Elaine started as she hugged Dyane's shoulders "a step away."

"A step away? From what?"

Dyane gasped.

"Oh my God" she answered her own question through the silence and tears of Karen and Elaine.

"Rusty sewed him up on the boat…" Elaine pointed out.

"Rusty?"

"Yeah, Rusty."

"Who the hell is Rusty? How does he know Jim?" said a startled and confused Dyane.

"Rusty is a woman…"

"A woman?" Dyane interrupted.

"Yeah…the captain's wife."

"The captain's wife?" she repeated. "What the fuck? I'm not following here."

"Dyane, Rusty came up from below and found her husband and your husband with bad injuries bleeding on the deck of the boat. She blew away Scott with one shot, and then tried to fix her husband and Jim's injuries. She stitched him up, but he developed a fever and infection. We have no idea how he's been able to hang on for so long."

"Oh my God."

"Yeah. But now something's going on outside and they are headed here…" said Karen.

Dyane snapped into reality for the moment.

"Oh my God. Jim is the one who hurt the captain?" Dyane asked to clarify.

"Yes." Both ladies answered simultaneously.

"Oh shit. That guy is coming here to kill Jim."

"That guy?" asked Elaine.

"Yeah. While I was looking for this place, I heard him leaving his house with those people and screaming about killing the guy who had just killed his brother, the captain."

"Oh shit" Karen agreed.

Dyane knelt at the side of the bed and leaned into her husband's side crying. She buried her face into his weakened chest and she blubbered uncontrollably.

Out of the blue, he moved his free arm from his heavily injured and infected side. He reached for her and laid that arm around her shoulder blades.

"Thank God" he whispered in her ear.

A moment later, Katmandu burst through the doorway still screaming with Rusty and Briggs in tow. He wasted no time.

He walked straight over to where Elaine, Karen and Dyane were. Dyane still had her head perched on Jim's chest and he was still holding onto her. The three women were crying.

"Is this the son of a bitch?" he yelled.

He held his sword high above Jim's ailing body.

The women standing gasped.

"NOOOOOOO!" screamed Dyane as she lay across Jim.

"Kat, don't do this!" demanded Rusty. "He's already dying! Don't do this!"

"NOOOOOOO!" screamed Dyane again.

Jewel turned over in Gianna's bed.

"WHAT ARE YOU DOING?" she screamed at him.

Jewel got up from the bed and walked over to the disturbance. The look on her face said it all.

"WHAT ARE YOU, FUCKING NUTS? HASN'T THERE BEEN ENOUGH DEATH? UNCLE, WHAT THE FUCK ARE YOU DOING?"

Katmandu paused with all of the drama from the women. He lowered his sword temporarily. He looked around as the room lightened. The looks on everyone's faces were easily made out.

To make everything even more chaotic, everyone started waking up on the slabs with the screaming taking place. With each passing second there were gasps and hushes and some horrifying shrieks.

Katmandu, in all of his urgency and impatience, cried out again "Is this the son of a bitch?"

He raised his sword over Jim.

Dyane didn't move. She was still kneeling at his side and lying across his chest.

Rusty stepped in front of Katmandu, between him and Jim and looked him square in the eyes. She felt his rage all too well. He knew her stubbornness as well.

"No, this is not the son of a bitch" she said in a monotone that meant nothing but business.

She stared into his eyes and he returned the favor. They were at a standstill.

More rustling took place around them, but the focus was most certainly on Katmandu and his sword arched high above Jim and Dyane.

There were more screams.

"Hey asshole! Over here!" came the loud scream from the doorway behind him.

Katmandu turned his attention to the doorway yet said nothing. His sword did not move.

"That's right asshole! I said over here…"

Katmandu became more agitated as he looked back at an ever weakening Jim and then over to the vocal Alan and silent Hunter. Alan had the look of fire all through him like he was energized from the almighty god Zeus himself.

"He didn't kill your brother."

Katmandu gave Alan his full attention…though stood there silent pondering his next move.

"I SAID…HE DIDN'T KILL YOUR BROTHER! ARE YOU HARD OF HEARING ASSHOLE?"

Katmandu was ready to attack. But being the shrewd warrior, he looked Alan over to ensure there was no trap awaiting his attack. There wasn't as far as he could tell.

Rusty moved into his way once again.

"No Kat, no."

Katmandu was breathing fire.

"Get out of my way" he commanded Rusty.

"No I will not."

"Are you disobeying me woman?" he demanded.

"Yes. He did not kill Bones."

"How would you know?"

"Because I know who killed him."

"And which one is it? Which one Rusty?" he demanded.

She wouldn't say. She stood like a statue yet filled with passion.

"Your silence is noted as is your loyalty. Get out of my way and I will kill them all!" he screamed.

"I am not moving Kat."

"Rusty, move or die!"

"Are you threatening me with death…your brother's wife…who is now in control of our destiny?" Rusty questioned logically.

Katmandu looked at her as he hesitated for his answer.

Obviously his rage had gotten the best of him as Rusty, with the passing of her husband Blackeye Bones, did assume the leadership role of the pirate family by their own charter. So he hesitated and quickly analyzed his next move knowing that there could be consequences.

Rusty stood steadfast.

"Lower your sword Kat" she firmly said again meaning business.

He stood there steadfast as well.

His voice much lower in tone, he warned her again.

"Move or die! This is family business! You know that!"

All eyes were on the power struggle, except Dyane's, whose eyes were closed still buried in the chest of Jim. Even Jim's eyes were focused as best as possible on Katmandu.

Rusty held her ground.

"Lower your sword. I will not say it again" she warned. "Don't push me."

Katmandu looked past Rusty to Alan. Alan was poised and ready for an attack. His stance was clear.

Katmandu then turned his attention to Jim. He saw how weak he was, and pretty much was convinced that he was his brother's killer. His concern was why would Rusty lie to him outright? He was not backing down because he wanted revenge and he was not to be denied the retribution he sought.

He looked back at Rusty, and then alternated between Briggs and Rusty. Rusty was not armed but Briggs had one arm on the handle of his sword and another on the handle of a gun. Briggs looked calm, though ready to make a move if needed to.

Katmandu took one last look at Rusty.

He made his move…

Chapter 18

The consequences were real. The screams were deafening.

But why did it come to this?

Why was Rusty seemingly on the side of the vacationers to begin with?

Katmandu did have a point and made it convincingly well…after all, they *are* pirates! And what do pirates do? Well, rape, plunder, pillage, kill… anything they damn well please!

Does anything matter though when even pirates make mistakes?

Mistakes? Pirates can **make mistakes**?

Before Rusty and Katmandu made it into the housing unit for the captives, there obviously was a power struggle throughout the journey that originated from Katmandu's house. Dyane was witness to pieces of it just prior to finding and entering the camp where her husband was.

That power struggle was a bit more than just the fact that Rusty's husband and Katmandu's brother, Captain Blackeye Bones, had died from injuries sustained by Jim Stowe, leader of the vacationers.

What else were they screaming about?

They were screaming about the fact that they had made a huge blunder in their plunder.

The yacht that they overtook was the wrong one.

The wrong one?

Oh yes.

The pirate plan was premeditated. They knew what they were out on the sea to do that particular day. And they executed the plan well. However, one thing got in the way.

The yacht that they were supposed to overtake and hijack was suppose to have two billionaire investors on it, none other than world traveler Cathleen Brassell-Jenkins and her husband Ron, and Bruce Griswold with his wife JoAnn. Both were huge profile couples in the world of business: Cathleen in the health field started as a lactation consultant and specialist who developed an extraordinary technique to help birthing mothers and their newborns; and JoAnn in the hospitality arena who made her fortune revolutionizing techniques for producing mass quantities of food safely in a sterile environment that was exponentially more successful than the current standards of the day. Both women than parlayed their small fortunes into massive riches utilizing their intelligence and savvy in the investment markets. The information that the pirates had obtained put the two billionaires on that exact boat coming out of that key at that exact time on that particular day.

The only issue was that the information was wrong. Fortunately for them, the wealthy couples and their party had delayed their pleasure trip for two weeks because of unforeseen circumstances, opening up the boat for Jim Stowe and his vacation group. The pirates, even though well recognized for their superb reputation in recognizance, never received that updated information.

So, instead of kidnapping two of the wealthiest people in the world with the potential for a huge money making ransom, the pirates were left with a group of average to above average income every day commoners just out for the trip, and adventure, of their lives. And boy, did they get just that...

That all added in to the passion and intensity of the confrontation between Rusty and Katmandu.

In simple terms after the loss of her husband, Rusty was all about releasing them. There were no plausible explanations to hold them, keep them, or ransom them. Moreover, she certainly didn't want to kill them.

Katmandu, after the loss of his brother, had a much different take on it. He not only wanted, but desired, revenge and death to them. He obsessed with pain, suffering, and slaughter. He turned into a one vision pirate out of control. And there was no one who was going to stop him.

Though, Rusty made it her mission to…

Katmandu did make his move. The consequences were real, and the screams were deafening.

It proved to be his last move.

In a flurry of moves reminiscent of a long boring game of chess going nowhere and then trading pieces in a passionate show of action, the scene shifted into utter chaos.

Katmandu had held his sword high above the dying Jim Stowe. His wife Dyane was blanketed on top of him, emotional from the fact of just seeing him moments earlier after being apart since the hijacking of their rented yacht.

With one split second, Katmandu lowered his sword feverishly into the lower gut of Jim Stowe, just missing Dyane by an inch or two. There was no doubt the result. Gurgling between blood and air, Stowe gasped his last breath and grabbed hold of Dyane's arm and whispered "I love you" through the gurgles.

She lost it.

Instead of being frozen with the shock of what just happened to her longtime spouse and life partner, upon hearing the final words from Jim, she did a one eighty roll before Katmandu could pull the sword from Jim, and flipped herself up onto her feet. In one continuous motion, she kneed the hostile pirate in his crown jewels making him double over gasping for breath. She then reached over and grabbed the sword from her husband's belly and shoved it into his neck and throat area as she shook with horror.

All of this before Rusty could grab the gun from Briggs and shoot him…which was Rusty's intention if he had made such a foolish move.

He made the move, Rusty made the move, but Dyane beat Rusty for the kill.

Dyane then collapsed.

There was pandemonium.

Screams, jumping, running all about were all prevalent. There were even some hushes and some 'oh my God' mumblings.

What a way to start the day?

Jewel sprinted over and hugged her mother Rusty so hard that Rusty nearly fell over. Jewel's terror was obvious.

Alan rushed in to help Dyane, who was lying on the floor partially on top of Katmandu. Summer raced over as well. Dyane was unconscious.

Rusty just stood there holding Jewel. She was speechless. Briggs was tongue tied too. In front of them lied the hulking figure of Katmandu bleeding out from a late, but heroic, stab from his own sword by the hands of his last victim's wife.

Jewel had lost total control. Between sobs she was alternating screaming and catching her breath. None of what she said could be made out, but she was muffling something into her mother's body every time she buried her face into a different body part. She was hyperventilating, yet Rusty did little to calm her down. She held Jewel, but she herself just stood there mesmerized.

It was an unnecessary turn of events. No one had to die. But now, there were pirates running everywhere tracking down the group of vacationers who just flipped out with the violence that occurred as they awoke from their dreams and/or nightmares.

As stated before, what a way to start a day…

Caleb and Dylan had fallen asleep for an hour or so next to the mine once again. After watching Dyane go off into the darkness, both yielded on any plans to catch her or find her in the thicket. They were way too exhausted to go anywhere as it was. So they both decided to sit tight and wait until dawn before making that supreme decision about what they would do next.

Strangely, they heard all of the commotion in the distance around dawn and beyond. They couldn't make out any words or ideas and such, but they heard the buzz from as far away as they were. Their curiosity peaked as the daylight was becoming closer to one hundred percent.

"So what do you think? Can we finally leave this shithole?" Dylan asked.

"About time you asked. I was waiting on you!" Caleb remarked sarcastically. "So what do you want to do with this mine?"

"Blow it up? Please? Please?" Dylan reacted childishly.

There was no doubt that either had had their fill of this situation, this island, and this vacation. There was an aire of slap happiness and a distinct odor of frustration and sarcasm. Both were honestly hoping that neither would say anything to piss the other off. Fortunate for both of them, each also checked their sensitivity at the entrance to the island.

"So blow it up! What the hell are you waiting for?" challenged Caleb.

"Really? Can I? Can I?" the childish act continued from Dylan.

"Look just do it. Don't be an ass about it. Just do it..." Caleb snapped.

"And then what?" Dylan went on.

"And then what?" Caleb repeated with irritation.

"Yeah. And then what?" Dylan echoed Caleb.

"And then I pick up your arms and your legs and carry all your pieces back to camp so Mandy can bury you in the sand. You dumb ass...you have no idea how powerful that thing is..."

"Can we see? Please? Please?" Dylan childishly questioned with a huge grin and wide eyes.

"What the hell is this...Ren and Stimpy meet Pee Wee Herman? Because this sure ain't Family Guy! Stewie would have kicked your ass by now. Shit, Kenny would have killed you in South Park by now...dude, shut the fuck up!"

Caleb gave him the death stare following his verbal tirade. Dylan paused to reflect on Caleb's level of aggravation.

Sheepishly, Dylan looked up at Caleb. With those innocent young eyes, he crossed eye beams with Caleb.

"Sorry, man" he apologized quietly. "I didn't mean to piss you off... really."

"Okay."

"But..." he said and paused...staying quiet for almost ten seconds...

"Can I still blow it up? Please? Please?" he went on in his best Pee Wee Herman impersonation.

Caleb looked at him unamused. Dylan laughed anyway. He was trying to keep from going insane. So was Caleb, but it was very understandable how patience had run out and bare nerves were beginning to show.

Caleb managed a dry smile.

"Dude, do what you want. Me? I don't need to see that thing blow up."

Okay Caleb, seriously, what do you want to do? Head back top camp? Go looking for Dyane? Both? Neither?" Dylan asked in a calm serious tone.

"Actually both. But before we do, what do you say we find their stash of speed boats so we can go back to camp with *something* to give them."

Dylan nodded in agreement.

Both got up and stretched their limbs, shaking off any remnants of their exhaustive hour of sleep. They heard more disturbances from the general direction of the village and camp, and that got them moving.

"I hope all that noise isn't signaling that something's wrong..." Dylan said.

"Oh no...I'm sure it's their celebration that they got off of the island... and without us..." Caleb replied dryly.

Dylan chuckled as Caleb shook his head.

"What? What?" Dylan asked.

"What? What? How about I can't figure out if you're playing with me or if you are really that stupid!"

Dylan calmed down after initially being insulted.

"Man, I'm sorry...really I am. I was just playing and dealing with everything...I guess that's my way of staying sane..." said Dylan.

Both guys started walking away from the tremendous mine. They were quietly talking to each other and forging ahead when without any warning; Dylan reached down, picked up a rock, and fired it at the mine. Mind you, they were only about forty feet away from the mine...

when...

"BOOM!"

Chapter 19

The explosion completely rocked the island, shaking the ground and quaking the trees for a significant stretch of time. It was immensely loud, signaling the kind of power that was behind it.

The camp, which was still in severe disarray from the moves just minutes earlier that led to the deaths of two leaders, stopped everything. Everyone halted in their spots and turned toward the direction where the explosion originated. Everyone looked toward the sky and all of the pieces of debris that appeared to be flying through it...looked like a massive flock of gulls under the spell of some psychedelic mushrooms...

Even Rusty looked toward the sky through her tears and pain.

"What the hell was that?" she posed rhetorically.

The shaking of the ground sent some eerie chills up and down her spine. It drew her concern. Of course, she didn't expect an answer, but one was forthcoming anyway.

"Sounds like someone just dropped a bomb on us..." Briggs said, breaking his statuelike shock from the recent festivities.

"You're a master of the obvious, Briggs" she replied.

Briggs snickered at the sarcasm.

"Also sounds like it came from the other side of the island. There were no signs of planes. Don't know if there are any boats on the other side... want me to take a few guys and check it out?"

"No, I want you to stay here and help get this mess cleaned up. Have Ramon and Razor clear these bodies. Send R-Tard, Silly Willy and Tibs to check out the explosion."

"Rusty, the three of them couldn't find a coconut if it fell from a tree and hit them in the head. If they were lucky, between them they would possess half a brain of a parrot."

"Send them anyway. Maybe this will turn out to be the best day of their lives" she commanded.

"Aye, Rusty."

Briggs left to carry out the wishes of Rusty, who was still standing in the same position holding onto her daughter Jewel.

"Mom, I'm scared. I can't take this anymore."

"What do you mean Jewel? You've always been the strong one in the family. Nothing phases you…" Rusty said maternally.

"Mom, you haven't noticed what I've been going through for such a long time…" she confessed. "I'm not the strong one, never was and never will be."

"Oh honey…" reassured Rusty.

"Mom, I can't take this anymore. Daddy's gone, Uncle Kat is dead. And these people are innocent people who did nothing wrong but paid for all of this with some of their lives. I can't take this! Mom…help me please!"

Jewel was still hyperventilating and out of control. But who could blame her.

Rusty was at a loss as to what to do next. She continued to hold her daughter as she sustained her hysterical nature.

Dyane was pretty much frozen in time following her knifing of Katmandu, staring at the body she had fallen upon when she passed out. Coming back to consciousness wasn't a blessing in the least bit. She opened her eyes and realized that everything was actually fact. She saw the deep red blood still flowing from the neck of her victim. She strained to elevate herself when she accidentally put her hand on her dead husband to try and steady herself, only to fall down in pain and disgust. It was a tough slap of reality to someone who had a front seat of participation in this whole scene.

Dyane climbed back to her feet and saw how bad off Jewel was, and somehow found the insane thing to do within the craziness of everything. She hugged Jewel, at first saying nothing, and then whispering reassurance.

That didn't sit well with Rusty. She turned her body and Jewel's so that it pushed Dyane away from her emotional daughter.

But Dyane didn't back away. Instead, she repositioned herself to again hug Jewel. Jewel was receptive, though utterly confused. In light of everything, why was Dyane hugging her? And what was she saying to her? No one could make anything out, though Dyane was still whispering to Jewel.

Rusty was silent. She was dealing with myriad emotions. These emotions not only dealt with the losses of family, and of all the pain and suffering of Jewel, but also what she herself was going through. These three days were not a bed of roses for Rusty. And now all of the events of the last few days had culminated into one of the biggest and heaviest sorrows of her life, and who was there to help her through it…or even just help at all? No one…

Mark rolled over in the sand of the island along the shore he was stranded on. He had all kinds of issues since he arrived there with his open wounds and sheer loneliness in the past face of incredible terror and heroism. Days had gone by and all he could muster were a few feeble attempts at washing his open wounds.

"Damn, I'd do anything for a Wilson volleyball…" he would joke with himself as he tried to maintain his sanity.

Well, the explosion from the pirate island was so massive that it woke him up as he slept on the shore of that glorified sandbar.

It not only managed to get him up, but seemingly sobered him up into the current reality.

He rolled around still wincing from his adventure and awoke in fright that something could be so loud and so close…or at least it **seemed** so close. He saw the smoke from the explosion and made the rash decision that he had to get there, no matter what. It didn't matter how sore he was or how much pain he was experiencing from his leap from the boat amidst bullets flying, he had to get there. The feeling inside of him grew instantly thinking that his friends were somehow connected to that explosion.

So without thinking any further, he struggled to get to his feet. He shook off the little sand crabs that were attached to him in some way and walked gingerly to the shoreline. He bent over at the waist and attempted to touch his toes. Every part of his body was tight, from the hamstrings in his legs to his skin that were in some places badly sunburned and blistery.

He stayed in that stretching position for about fifteen seconds, feeling somewhat good that he was getting the feeling going in his legs, yet struggling with that nasty sunburn. He repeated the stretching moves and added a few more, somehow dealing with the skin agony.

And although quite dehydrated and to a point a little lightheaded from malnourishment, he walked into the early morning warm water. The open wounds were still not accepting of his decision, but had no choice but to go along with the rest of his adrenaline filled body in search of his friends.

He walked in the water for about five minutes or so, getting used to the feeling of it surrounding his skin. In some ways it was a cool feeling of soothiness, yet in other ways, it was downright painful. But being a past swimmer in school and junior Olympic team competitions, he put all that discomfort behind him and focused on the task at hand.

He began to swim.

Mark stayed close to the shore for a few minutes as he continued to stretch his muscles in the water by swimming in differing strokes.

And with a determination that only can be felt at championship levels, he took off in the direction of the smoke filled the sky. He had that burst of energy, but just how long it would physically last was the only concern. He was not familiar with the area, where the sandbars were positioned for rest, or the much deeper shipping lanes which could be his major challenges with currents. He was not prepared to be swimming such a journey in the Caribbean Sea for it was a much different challenge than, say, swimming in an Olympic size pool against a competitor. And mentally, could he stay headstrong in the face of a possibly deteriorating physical condition?

Oh…and…where are the sharks and barracudas?

He didn't think about anything else but his friends.

So he swam.

R-Tard led the small contingent of manpower through the jungle to investigate the unexpected explosion. There were no planes buzzing overhead, and the views that they had of the inlet and the seas on the other side of the island were all clear of any ships. The timing of the explosion shortly after dawn made the explosion that much more unbelievable.

But the dark smoke and ensuing fire in the jungle bore proof that the unexpected did actually happen.

The pirate trio made it to the outskirts of the smoke and fire in about fifteen minutes. They had no firefighting gear or breathing apparatus to use, so they cautiously moved around the boundaries of smoke and flame ensuring that they wouldn't trap themselves in the middle of it.

While sidestepping as much as they were able to, they made a couple of startling discoveries accidentally. Silly Willy walked right into one and tripped over it, falling into the thick brush.

"W-w-what ar dese?" R-Tard asked the others.

"No idea, man" replied Tibs. "But they look pretty serious."

"I w-w-wunda" R-Tard continued "dey look like bombs of some kind..."

"They are fucking huge, man..." Tibs answered. "I ain't never seen these before. They're bigger than the old cannonballs we have..."

"Yeah" Silly Willy responded in awe. "Look at their shape...they look like they have arms..."

They had discovered a handful of mines close to the original explosion. There was no sign of human life around the area that they were in. The mines weren't sitting out in an obvious way, all were somewhat covered with jungle growth. But they were still mines nonetheless.

One would have thought that the pirate civilization would have found these on routine walks through the jungle, but it was quite clear that R-Tard, Silly Willy and Tibs had not done so. Fact is they had never seen a mine to begin with. So they were curious to the dark metal objects with the funny looking arms.

Their curiosities brought them closer to the mines. But they weren't as cautious as maybe they needed to be.

Silly Willy and Tibs went right up to one, uncovered the vines and brush from it and began to touch it and prod it. R-Tard stayed a good twenty feet away showing apprehension.

"Guys, be caireful. We don't know anything ab-b-bout dem..." R-Tard commanded.

"No problem, man..." Tibs said as he still poked and prodded the object.

BOOM!!

The explosion was as loud as the first one, but seemed closer to where everyone was situated in the prisoner area.

Pieces of pirates went flying through the air like they had just been launched from a rocket launcher from NASA. Those pieces had quite an excellent distance to them, some making their way all the way to camp. Remnants of arms and hands and torsos landed not far from the camp, and the cloud of smoke was similar to the initial blast that originated the search journey.

The ground shook some more. Pieces of brush and jungle also flew to the camp area. The fireball was easily seen and lasted just an instant.

Rusty had seen enough.

"Everyone battle stations! Some one or some thing is out there! And they are getting closer! Everyone else take cover!" Rusty ordered.

The initial chaos hadn't quite subsided as yet when the second one took place. The second chaos was insane.

Pirates ran back to the village. Pirates ran to the huge wooden row boats tied to the shoreline to make sure they were secured. And yet others ran for the secret area where they housed their speed boats and modern weapons.

The captives?

They were left standing there in disbelief. Or some decided to run for the water and try to swim to the pirate ship or the yacht anchored well offshore in the inlet. That plan didn't get very far for the few who did try and escape that way. Whether it was the sheer terror of what just happened or the mystery of the unknown, all of the captives attempting that got only so far into the water and paused. It could have been the group of pirates running to their row boats that made them stop. No one really knew.

Rusty grabbed hold of Jewel and they both scampered back to their house in the village. That was quite a distance away, and Rusty ensured that neither wasted any time in doing so.

Ramon and Razor left Katmandu's body in the sand and took off for their battle station. Briggs took off with Rusty and Jewel for their protection in case it was really an attack of some kind.

Dyane was left standing alone in shock as all she had to look at was either the cloud of smoke in the sky or her husband's torn and tattered body. She was speechless with little movement...just standing there. No one really noticed her standing there in all of the commotion as all of the captives had either moved for cover inside the building where they already were or attempted an escape of some kind. Those who chose to stay inside the building could really only hide under the wooden slabs.

There was a lot of background noise. A lot of people were breathing heavy, or just labored with the overwhelming emotion that came with each blast.

And like a total oddity in the face of the events, a lone woman raced from under one of the wooden beds and ran to Dyane. She took hold of Dyane with both hands on her arms and looked at her straight in the eyes and blurted out "I hope Dylan is okay…" as she stood there in shock.

Another word was not heard or said. They stood there for what must have seemed like an eternity when Alan raced in and grabbed both of them immediately ushering them under a raised wooden slab.

"Come on ladies, take cover" Alan said.

The ladies just stared out into the abyss.

The second blast sent Mark into an instant stoppage in the sea. The vibrations could be felt through the air as well as the water. It was an unusual feeling of rumbles going through his lower body that was submerged below sea level.

Mark had made some decent time as he was stroking towards the site of the first explosion when the second one took place.

Unfortunately for Mark, the sea life scattered away from the island and some came directly into his path. Those sea life creatures included all kinds of fish, including barracudas and sharks…

He tried to swim forward following his pause from the second blast. The obstacles proved too great…

Chapter 20

Boom!

BOOM!!

KABOOM!

*T*hree more massive explosions took place about forty five seconds after the second one. Their sensitivity sensors proved to be sensitive all right.

And yet while Dylan was responsible for setting off the first one with a harmless throw of an object from forty to fifty feet, and Silly Willy and Tibs could be easily blamed for the second one, the only thing left to assign the responsibility for the other blasts were the shock waves or something similar that could trigger the other three mines.

By now, half of the island was in flames. The pirates maintained their stations awaiting word otherwise. That is, the pirates who were still alive.

The last trio of explosions was strong enough to level some of the pirate village. Houses collapsed on people. And no one was there for any rescues. The pirates who were still alive were well armed and ready for whatever enemy was out there to blow them away.

Still, the enemy never showed themselves.

While the pirates were in red alert mode, the captives were unsure of their next move. With all of the explosions and the fierceness of them, all turned afraid to make any bolder moves of escape.

The fifth blast rocked the captive's sleeping quarters so intensely that debris started caving in from the roof. The only thing saving those vacationers at the moment was those sturdy heavy wooden slabs they called beds.

The fear was present, passionate and all accounted for.

Each minute was like an hour to every single one of them.

Burning tree branches and jungle debris landed in the prisoner compound. The fire could be seen from the area. And yet no one could move to help their situation.

The fire expanded throughout the island as time wore on. The morning blasts and smoke could be heard and seen from other islands in the distance, but were there anyone there to witness them?

And as time moved forward, more explosions ruled the island. The sixth blast was a series of explosions as the fires had reached the pirate marina where their modern day speedboats were docked. They were not mines, but the gas tanks associated with those boats.

As those explosions took place, another large part of the pirate village came crumbling down. Pirates who were manning a battle station at the docks were killed instantly by the series of explosions. Those speed boats went up in flames as did the docks.

The pirates who were still alive then made a run from their village to their large row boats not far from the prisoner compound. Their concerted effort to get off the island was going well for the moment until another large explosion took place from yet another mine, with pieces of that mine showering the compound, the shore and the inlet area. It was the sixth mine to erupt unannounced.

To the dismay of the eight or so pirates in one of the boats, a large chunk of white hot mine landed in the middle of the boat taking out all eight of them instantly. The two men and six women had just reached the boat and were getting situated when the blast took place and the uninvited chunk decimated the vessel.

That left one boat that was filled with what looked like sixteen pirates made up of four men, six women and six children. It didn't appear that Rusty, Jewel or Briggs were with them. Most were in some phase of urgent hysterics, especially the women and children. The men were rowing for dear life.

Their direction was the only floating ships left, the pirate ship and the rented yacht.

The challenge was in front of them. Each knew the consequences that could take place as flaming debris was also raining down throughout the lagoon and around each of the boats.

The whole scene was pandemonium.

And it appeared as though the vacationers were to be trapped on the burning island.

The sleeping quarters did collapse with the sixth mine detonating. From anywhere within a couple of miles of the island, anyone could have sworn that the island had a volcano erupting.

But there was no one within that distance that witnessed it. Or was there?

Most of the group of first time adventurists was buried alive by the collapse. The moans and groans of people suffering and in pain were heard throughout. But none of those could be reached. The few who did escape the rubble tried in vain to free some of the others, but they couldn't and tried to free themselves from the island.

Rushing out of the collapsed mess of wood and stone were Alan, Hunter and Elaine. They ran out of the one time structure saying prayers.

They each got as far as the water line when another mine blew loud and clear.

Alan stopped and turned toward the rubble.

"I can't leave them..." he said.

"I know how you feel, Alan, but we were in there. We all know that nothing else could have been done..." Hunter said putting an arm around Alan's shoulder.

"But I can't leave them..." Alan mumbled again. "I know you're right, but I can't leave them."

"Dude, that's suicide. Come on, let's get swimming..." replied Hunter.

"As much as I don't want to die, I still can't leave them..." Alan went on. "You guys go. Swim fast. I want to make one more check. Heck if I can get even one person out, that's one more than right now..."

"You sure? You want me to stay with you?" Hunter asked.

"No, take Elaine and go. You have each other. Swim. I already lost Scotty. I have no one now. Go quickly. I need to get back in there…"

Hunter hugged Alan. Elaine did as well.

Alan made the first move and ran back to the piles of wood and stones. Hunter and Elaine looked at each other in pause and then agreed to go. They turned and ran into the water coming up in full swim stride. They had the same challenges ahead as the one row boat that was now about halfway to the pirate ship with the addition of one other…they were swimming.

Alan got to the debris quickly and started tossing wood and stone away from the collapsed structure. He made some pretty decent headway to the voices that were still alive but trapped.

The fires were edging closer and could easily be seen from the prisoner camp. The smoke was thick and black and could be seen for miles.

Suddenly, there was another tremendous explosion from the pirate village. Most of the village was now going up in flames and the smells of burning wood, metal, and life were permeating the camp.

Alan turned nauseas and tried to keep his stomach. But the smells became stronger and stronger. He held steadfast, bending to move the structure materials. He got to a wooden slab and freed two of the girls, Gianna and Eryan. Both were hurt, but both were able to assist Alan in moving some wood and rock to try to get to other wooden slabs. Although all of the slabs were buried by now, there were some air pockets that were keeping some of the captives alive.

"Help! Someone help!" was heard above the moans…

"Anyone out there? Help me please!" was another.

Alan answered them.

"Hang on, I'm trying to get to you…" he shouted in support back. "Hang on…"

Gianna and Eryan were not succeeding as well as first hoped. Although both were trying, both were hurt and weak. Alan understood their issue.

"Ladies, go swim to the boat. Can you both do that?"

"I don't think so…we're both hurt on our sides" Gianna said. "We will still try and help though…"

Alan smiled and thanked them for their effort and support.

All three turned their attention to moving boulders again when another explosion took place. Again, debris came showering upon them in the camp.

This time they were not so lucky.

A large chunk of metal rained down right on top of them, crushing any further efforts…

Chapter 21

The fire continued to burn out of control eventually enveloping the entire island. Explosions of mines were heard throughout the rest of the day.

With the same explosion that put the finishing touches on any rescue intentions in the captive's camp, part of the shrapnel shower also came down onto the last of the pirate row boats, splitting the boat into several pieces and fatally wounding all sixteen aboard.

Hunter and Elaine were not so lucky as well. Both swam into some burning debris that encircled about a twenty foot area that was floating in their path. Neither saw the debris and ended up swimming into it and becoming trapped by it...

Both sustained extensive burns from swimming right into the fire, but both managed to stay afloat, and alive, while each improvised their next moves.

"Elaine, you okay? Are you still with me?" Hunter cried out, not able to see her in the water.

"Yeah, I'm still here. Burned but okay...you?"

"I'm good. Stay with me as best as you can. We'll get through this" promised Hunter. "We're gonna have to swim under this stuff. Are you okay to do this?"

"Yes, I think so" she answered with a quivering voice.

The truth of the matter was that Elaine was weakening quickly and wasn't sure how much further she could go. They still had a good one hundred yards or so just to get to the yacht. Then they would have to figure out how they were going to get aboard.

"Honey, just don't leave me behind" she called out.

Hunter never heard her. He went underwater and started swimming beneath the debris that surrounded them.

She saw that he left, and then tried to do the same. She was badly burned on her left wrist, arm and side, the skin already broken, open and getting more painful by the second. She grasped as much breath as she could and went underwater. She swam in the same direction as her husband, but just wasn't as strong with her stroke or her lung capacity to hold on as long as he could.

He easily made it under the wreckage to the other side. He came up, wiped his face and looked all around for her. She was no where to be found.

He waited ten seconds, peering around in anticipation for her to surface.

He saw nothing but burning trees, wood and metal.

Hunter filled his lungs with air and submerged himself under water. With eyes open, he swam back in retracing his strokes in hopes of finding Elaine. The water was about sixteen feet deep where they were and for the most part clear, so he figured finding her would not be that much of a challenge.

It wasn't.

He found her struggling to stay afloat. However, there was one small issue. She resurfaced in the middle of some burning materials. She was writhing in pain as her legs were paddling out of control.

Seeing this, Hunter came up quickly.

"Elaine, hang on. I'm coming to get you. Be ready to hold your breath. I'm going to pull you under and get you out of there!" he screamed.

He could hear her crying loudly with pain.

Once again, he went under water and swam to his wife. Knowing he had no room to surface, he took her by the hips and pulled her down hoping that she had heard him and was ready to escape her situation. Luckily, she was. What he didn't count on was how lifeless she had become.

He was hoping that once he guided her out of harms way that she would be able to resume her pace toward the yacht. His hopes were not answered.

He was able to guide her safely to the other side of the trouble when another explosion showered the surrounding area with more pieces and parts of burning and smoldering carnage from the jungles. Thankfully, nothing hit them or came even remotely close to them.

Hunter held his wife in his arms as they surfaced and he waded to stay afloat. She was conscious but too weak to depend upon herself. So it was time for him to carry them both.

"Hang on, Honey, this will be a bumpy ride, but we'll make it" he told her.

She smiled through the pain at him.

Hunter shook off the pain from his burns and held her as he swam toward the yacht. It was a long enough swim under normal conditions, but now he had burns over a good part of his right side, and he was also carrying another person with him. She was best described as dead weight, which is difficult enough to be swimming with, yet much easier than having that weight flailing around.

He stuck to his plan of being patient and pacing his strokes as best as possible.

He also did a lot of praying at that time…which included a promise to Jesus about being a model Catholic if He helped them get through this. He asked forgiveness, but that was not about to come easy.

Hunter was about twenty five yards from the boat when another explosion rocked the island. His stick-to-itiveness was to be commended, though he was weakening as his pace slowed. He was running out of gas and his arm strength was about zero when he looked up to the skies.

"Please Lord! Please! Give me the strength!" he cried out.

Elaine could sense things slipping away in a hurry.

She whispered "I love you Hunter…forever" as she felt herself letting go.

Hunter struggled to hold onto her. Still, he felt Elaine slipping away.

The water was simply too much: the depth, the waves and current, and the burning debris. Elaine was just too much: her weight upon his tired frame. And his injuries were just too much: his burns and his loss of stamina.

And with one more stride, one more stroke, he was ready to go under himself. He made his peace with God, though it wasn't a pleasant one. He truly wanted to survive, with Elaine, and he pleaded his case silently to Him. No signs were returned.

As his energy left him from yet another stroke, still some fifteen yards away from the yacht, there was a lifeline thrown.

Hunter's arm hit a piece of wood that was bobbing and floating in the sea. It wasn't just a piece of driftwood that measured four by four inches from a dock or anything like that. It was a sturdy piece of wood that was much larger. It must have measured about two feet across and about four feet long. But what was more important, was that it was thick and sturdy and floating.

He held onto that piece of wood with one arm, being able to rest himself upon it while holding onto a still conscious Elaine.

"Honey…Elaine…I need you to help me with this. Do you have any strength left in your arms?"

"I'm not sure. I can't even feel one of them anymore."

"Elaine, I need you to see if you can hold onto this piece of wood. Please. It will help me rest my arms for awhile and then we can make it to the boat."

"Are we close Hunter?"

"Yeah…about fifty feet or so…real close. Come on Lainey, let's not give up now. Dig deep…please!"

Elaine moved her left arm from Hunter and slipped into the water further going under.

He grabbed her and positioned her onto the wood while getting her face above water. It was an epic struggle, but Hunter was not to be denied.

Elaine held onto the board while struggling for air. She then found her comfort zone and relaxed a bit while holding on.

Hunter then did the same, giving his arms a chance to rest.

"Good job Lainey…we're almost there" he smiled at her.

"Thank God. I don't know how much more I can take" she said smiling back.

While the rest time went by, both said prayers together in hopes that it would strengthen them spiritually enough to help support themselves mentally and physically for the last fifteen yards and then a climb onto the yacht.

They let fifteen minutes go by as they clung onto the wood. The current was taking them away from the yacht, but Hunter did some kicking with his legs to make sure they didn't lose the distance that they had already had.

Following their extended prayers, they came to the decision that it was time. The boat was so close, yet they were so far away.

They could both see the island deteriorating in front of their eyes. The fires had spread now to one hundred percent of the island. What was once full of life was now a death trap for anyone still alive on it.

Before they left that piece of wood, they both had a moment of silence and another prayer for their friends.

"Lainey, we gotta do this for them as well as for us…" Hunter said with determination.

"Okay, let's do this" she replied.

They let go of the wood and with all available strength, both Elaine and Hunter swam toward the yacht. Elaine had rested long enough that she was able to go solo, but she had no idea for how long. With her arm and side open and raw, that pain had long ago become numb…her arm and side almost completely useless to her. So she stroked the best that she could one armed, using her legs to move the distance.

Hunter was never more than two arms length away, making sure that he didn't lose her if she weakened suddenly. His patience in all of this was tremendous.

Both reached the back of the boat where the challenge was formidable but not overwhelming to climb onto the back platform and pull themselves up. Hunter went first, but not before securing Elaine to the edge of the platform. He thought it would be much more successful to pull her up from a stable position than to push her up from the water while trying to stay afloat. He was right.

The whole process took a few minutes and both smiled and hugged each other as they stood upon the platform. One last climb over the back of the boat and they were set.

This time Hunter guided Elaine up and over the back wall using the ladder and he followed suit. Seconds later they both collapsed on padded seats with smiles on their faces thanking God for His help.

And time slipped away…

Chapter 22

*T*ime did go by…hours and hours with no movement from the James couple.

Time slipped by…days and days…and there was no movement from anyone, whether on the yacht or the island.

Hunter awoke first and surveyed the situation. He had no idea that days had drifted by while he and Elaine were passed out in their seats. Lucky for them, those padded seats were underneath an awning, so the brutal Caribbean sun played no part in hurting them any further.

He looked over his burns and open wounds to assess how bad he was. He deemed himself fine.

He then looked at Elaine, and saying a thankful prayer that she was breathing while passed out in her seat. He looked over her burns and open wounds. They were not in good shape, though they weren't as severe as what he had first thought. He let her sleep. He figured if he could get this boat moving, that she would be very treatable back on the mainland.

He then looked over to the island and saw a smoldering mess. He also saw what looked like a deserted pirate ship next to theirs. But his concern was finding the way he could get this yacht moving.

Hunter stood up and wandered around the boat. All he could do was shake his head in disbelief as around every corner popped up another memory from what had happened originally on the boat.

"Unbelievable" he said over and over.

As he surveyed the boat, he noticed quite a bit of damage to parts of it. The flying debris from the explosions didn't spare the yacht at all. Although the yacht had not erupted in fires, there were some areas with holes in the decks and smoldering pieces of metal and wood.

Once again shaking his head, his level of urgency pushed on.

"Figures" he said when looking at some of the damage. "Hope the engines work…"

He made his way to the engine room area and immediately didn't like what he saw.

"Shit."

The area had taken a direct hit from some metal debris and it didn't appear as though the engines would ever start. Hunter was not a 'grease man' or engine man by trade. With minimal knowledge of engines to begin with, he had no idea what to look for, especially with boat engines.

That didn't deter him from poking around, but it was all foreign to him.

He then recapped the situation.

"Vacation of a lifetime, hijacked by pirates, held captive, death and starvation, daring escapes and now stranded. Man, I could write a book about this…if it ever ends!" he laughed sarcastically.

Then, overcome with emotion and fatigue, Hunter went back to the seats where he and his wife Elaine had occupied the previous few days and sat down. He dozed off.

Once again, days elapsed…

Chapter 23

Captain Mike Zgrabik left port with first officer Doreen Knaser out of Paradise Key with a crew of two more. On their expansive yacht they had a total of fourteen people, most notable the billionaires Cathleen Brassell-Jenkins and JoAnn Griswold and their group of eight others. The five couples were to enjoy a week of sailing through the Caribbean, stopping by tiny islands and ports for adventures and shopping.

With Doreen at the helm, Captain Mike played the fine host to his guests, ensuring that everyone was comfortable with their quarters and had refreshments as they slowly sped out south of the Keys.

It was another beautiful day, and the string of beautiful days down in that area was now at least three weeks long.

While chatting up with Cathy and JoAnn, Mike came across some interesting information.

"I know you put together this trip at the last minute with us, but how was it that you came to us for this adventure?"

"Well, originally we were supposed to charter our own yacht. We had a staff ready to sail it and we had a specific agenda to hold ourselves to" explained Cathy.

"Yeah, that's right" JoAnn agreed. "Remember what happened that we had to postpone?"

"I think it was one of us who had an emergency commitment or something so we put it off a week or two. Then we found out we could go, and when we came back to recharter the boat, I guess they had rented it out already to a large group coming from all over the country" Cathy said.

"Really?" asked Mike. "Are you talking about the yacht *"Forever"*?"

"Yeah, that's it. That was the name of the boat. Why?" Cathy questioned.

"Well, we have no idea what happened to it" Mike shared.

"What do you mean?" inquired JoAnn.

"Well, from what I heard, the boat sailed off with that group. It was never heard from again."

"That's right..." Cathy nodded "because when I went back to make sure that everything was set for us when they returned, I was told that they had disappeared."

"Did they say what happened?" Mike asked.

"No, no clue is what I was told. They had booked the boat for a specific adventure...you know...one of those pirate adventures or something...and they were never heard from again..." replied Cathy.

"No kidding..." Mike said.

Captain Mike excused himself from the conversation and headed up toward Doreen at the helm.

"Hey Doreen, did you hear about the "Forever" yacht that never came back?"

"Yeah, I heard about it. Damn shame."

"Heard what? What do you know?" Mike asked.

"I just heard what people were saying, that's all. The boat never came back. Some people said that they just sailed away with it, while others think that it was just another tourist accident and it went down. Either way, it's a shame. Hurts our business and reputation down here..."

"Did you hear anything about a pirate adventure with that boat?" Mike pushed.

"I heard something about that, but I really don't know. Why?"

"Just a hunch, but have we heard from Bones at all in the past few weeks?"

"Bones? No...why?" she asked.

"Weren't they doing some pirate production of some kind?"

Doreen looked distant, and then refocused quickly.

"I don't know...I'm not sure..."

"Yeah, I'm not sure either..." Mike conceded. "But you know what?"

"What?" Doreen hinted.

"We have a little time here...what you say we take a little detour and check that possibility out?" Mike stated.

"You're the Captain...you tell me. I'll head there if you want."

"Yeah...just a hunch..." he said.

"What kind of hunch?" she asked him.

"Not sure…yet. Let's swing by there for shits and giggles."

"Swing by where?"

"I think I know where he was planning to do this. It's way out in the middle of nowhere. No one ever heads there, so it would be perfect for such an adventure. Just don't know if it ever came to fruition with him…"

"Okay with me…"

Captain Mike gave her the coordinates and Doreen headed in that direction. The Guests had absolutely no idea what was going on as they were enjoying a nice scenic yacht ride through the tiny islands of the Caribbean.

A good hour or so later, Captain Mike noticed the smoldering ruins of an island in the distance. He was mingling with the Guests talking football with Ron Jenkins and Bruce Griswold and excused himself. He headed back to Doreen with a bounce in his step.

"Do you see what I see?" he asked her.

"Yeah. What do you make of it?"

"I don't know. But right now it concerns me. Big time concern" he said.

"Yeah. I can see why. There's no reason for an island to look like that. It looks like it's totally destroyed."

"That it does, Doreen, that it does. Let's keep this steady as she goes and let's head towards it."

"Shall I call the Coast Guard?" she asked.

"We're out of their jurisdiction, but we may want to call someone as we get closer. Hell, if it's a bad case scenario, I would say call them first and have them redirect us. But let's wait and see what is going on before we get others involved. If it's just a lightning fire or something, we would look pretty stupid…"

"Yeah, they certainly don't like false alarms…" agreed Doreen.

The island continued to get larger and larger as they approached it. As it neared, Cathy and JoAnn both made their way to Captain Mike.

"What's going on?" Cathy asked.

"We have a little time Cathy. We need to check something out…" he began.

"Check something out? Mike, we're not paying you to 'check something out'" interrupted JoAnn.

"Well ladies, in mentioning the boat 'Forever', you kind of just did…" said Mike.

"What do you mean?" JoAnn pushed back.

"Well, with your information you gave me earlier coupled with what Doreen here had heard, there might have been an issue that we need to check out."

"But…" interrupted a pushy JoAnn.

"And from what I see dead ahead, we may have some of those answers to the questions earlier. If something had happened to them, it's up to us to find out and report it. If lives are in danger…" eluded Mike.

"Jo, let them check. If that was us there, I certainly would want Captain Mike to check it out…" Cathy directed. "And we have extra time, so what's the hurt?"

JoAnn nodded in agreement.

"Doreen, take us closer and then around the island. Let's check out the lagoon inlet."

"Aye, Captain."

The decimation was very obvious. Captain Mike Zgrabik's boat got painfully close to the burned ruins that were evident. They had approached from the side of the island that several of the mines were situated and had exploded. What was once the jungle area was now just a shell of broken and burned trees and black charred ground.

The Guests were all curious, though hushed.

Doreen took them around towards the west and saw much of the same. On the southwest side of the island was the opening to the inlet.

They approached it very cautiously.

"It's obvious something happened here" Mike said to Doreen, Cathy and JoAnn. Ron and Bruce joined them.

"What's going on?" Ron asked.

"Ssshhh…" his wife said, waving her hand. "I'll tell you in a few minutes…"

The opening of the lagoon bore all kinds of driftwood and floating metal debris that was caught inside its boundaries.

"Yep…this was no lightening strike" Mike said. "There's something terribly wrong here."

The boat slowed as they reached the narrow opening to the inlet. Off to the left and coming into view was the pirate ship. The Guests could be heard reacting to seeing it. The ship was somewhat majestic in its tradition and a real eye catcher.

Moments later, they hit treasure.

"Oh my God…that looks like…yeah…it looks like the "Forever"…" Mike announced.

"Yes sir…that's the "Forever" all right…" confirmed Doreen.

"That's the boat that we were supposed to take?" Cathy asked.

"Yes it is" answered Mike. "Wow, look at all this damage everywhere."

Doreen slowed the yacht to almost a crawl.

"Yes, it's time Doreen. Notify the Coast Guard. There's something terribly wrong here."

"Aye."

"Cathy, we need to go in and check things out. You and the rest of the Guests can stay here, but I need to check this out…"

JoAnn was not motivated to do so.

"I understand" said Cathy. "Do what you need to do."

Mike picked up the radio and called for his crew of two to meet him. They both were there in a heartbeat.

"Guys, we need to take a look. You game?"

"Yes Captain…" they echoed.

"I'll have Doreen get us right up to the Forever and we'll try and board. My God, look at this lagoon…all the wreckage. Looks like several bombs went off here!"

Doreen finished her radio call to the Coast Guard and turned her attention back to Mike.

"Shall I get us right up to her Captain?"

"Yes, as close as possible. Coast Guard filled in?"

"Yes."

"Did you tell them of possible loss of life and in search of possible life?"

"Yes. They are on their way."

"Good. Take us to the back of the boat."

Doreen performed her magic and maneuvered to the back of the Forever. There were no signs of anything.

Captain Mike took himself and his two deckhands with him and boarded the disabled boat.

"Here…" he said as he discovered the two bodies sitting in the padded chairs under the awning. They were Hunter and Elaine James.

Mike checked for pulses immediately. Both were very weak but alive. He didn't move them.

"Tell Doreen to call for Lifeflight. We have two alive so far."

"Aye."

Mike noticed that both were dehydrated.

"Find me a couple of towels and get them wet…bring them here asap!" he ordered the other deckhand.

"Aye sir!"

Mike got up and looked around the ship quickly. He saw the damages from the original take over, though he didn't know anything about it.

"My God, there looks like there was quite a fight here…and blood stains. This is not good…" he said aloud.

The deckhand returned with damp towels that Mike quickly positioned on the forehead, face and neck of the two weakened people. Both of them moved slightly.

"Ssshhh…we're here to help. Hang on, you will be saved" Mike told them.

Hunter managed a small smile.

Captain Mike made sure the two in their seats were set before leaving them for the deck below. There he found no signs of life. He saw the engine area and the damages there.

He came back to the two passengers and stayed with them until the Lifeflight arrived minutes later.

The rescue was complete and Hunter and Elaine were being transported back to the mainland.

The Coast Guard arrived a few minutes after the Lifeflight helicopter had left.

There, it was a matter of the Coast Guard investigating the island and looking into the theories of what had occurred.

For Captain Mike and his crew, they were heroes for saving two lives and alerting the Coast Guard to what they discovered.

But before exiting the Forever, while going through the boat, he had found a pamphlet in one of the cabin rooms below deck. He looked at it as though he was studying for a test.

He then shook his head.

It was a tourist pamphlet about having a real life sea adventure with Pirates…

Captain Blackeye Bones and his crew…

Experience a sea jacking…and an island adventure…and eventually a treasure hunt and confrontation…all set to real life…

…and sailing out of Paradise Key…

…all describing to have the time of your life…

The End.

Epilogue

The Coast Guard did arrive and scour the island looking for survivors and clues to exactly what happened and how it happened.

What they found was a lot of dead bodies and an island that was charred beyond any reasonable theory could take them. In other words, they really couldn't come to a conclusion.

Eventually with the help of many local citizens who live in or around Paradise Key, the Coast Guard did put together a theory. Exhaustive interviews with the owner of the boat 'Forever' as well as interviews with Cathleen Brassell-Jenkins and JoAnn Griswold were fruitful.

Continued investigations on the island led to the discoveries of other mines that did not explode during the days of fire and destruction. As soon as those mines were found, the investigation went dark and closed. To this day, the actual file for this experience cannot be obtained or opened. But what was leaked out and/or told to the media following the events were deemed unofficial and hearsay.

Other theories did surface. One in particular dealt with terrorism. Another dealt with it being an off shoot to the Somali Pirates off the eastern coast of Africa.

Those theories and any others took all of three days to tear apart as Hunter and Elaine James slowly began their trek to becoming healthy again. Their account of what had happened though was so bizarre that the Coast Guard originally disregarded it as made up.

The infuriated couple then decided to stick it to the Coast Guard and every other nonbeliever by putting a book together of their experience, which led to a four movie deal with Fractured Pictures out of North Dakota. Both Hunter and Elaine are now rich beyond their means and are also now capable for paying for their five times a week therapist appointments.

They have not sailed ever again.

Cast of Characters

The Twenty Two Vacationers:

Jim Stowe	Captain of a rental yacht from Blaine, Min
Dyane Stowe	Wife of Jim
Hunter James	Childhood friend of Stowe, from Lynbrook, NY
Elaine James	Wife of Hunter
Joe Mont	Friend of Stowe, from Stuart, Fla
Karen Mont	Wife of Joe
Alan Mayes	Very close friend of Stowe, from Bay City, Mi
Scott Mayes	Alan's brother, from Saginaw, Mi
Dylan Dodge	Young friend of Stowe and James and newlywed, from Lynbrook, NY
Mandy Dodge	Wife of Dylan
Summer Sheridan	In Nursing school, from Blaine, Minnesota and family friend of the Stowe's. Daughter of Jessie
Jessie Sherman	Dyane's school friend from Pennsylvania
Chrissy	Dyane's school friend from Pennsylvania
Brandon Logue Young	Young family friend of the Stowe's from Ohio
Mark Russell	A best friend of Logue, also from Ohio
Eryan Bangs	College friend of Summer Sheridan from Minneapolis.
Gianna Anthony	College friend of Summer/Eryan from Blaine
Caleb Aquilino	From Annapolis, Md. Young friend of Jim. Big hulking guy in size, former Army Specialist
Kathleen Aquilino	Wife of Caleb.
Sean the Cop	From Annapolis, MD. Friend of several in the Group.

171

Others:

Cathleen Brassell Jenkins	Billionaire investor from Ohio
Ron Jenkins	Husband of Cathleen
JoAnn Griswold	Billionaire investor from Ohio
Bruce Griswold	Husband of JoAnn
Captain Mike Zgrabik	Captain of chartered boat service
Doreen Knaser	First Officer of Zgrabik's boat

The Pirates:

Blackeye Bones	Captain
Briggs	Second in command
Ratface	Very tall, very thin, the ugliest
Rusty	Captain Bone's wife
Razor	Pirate with muscle
Jewel	Daughter of Bones and Rusty, young, beautiful, somewhat overweight, possessing two teeth made of jewels, and owning the skills of a streak of meanness with a smile, tough appearing to be a late teen who is vulnerable
Ramon	Pirate with muscle
Silly Willy	Pirate known for his silliness and stupidity
R-Tard	Pirate with a stutter
Ripper	Pirate
Tibs	Pirate with long scar across chest
Katmandu	Pirate, Blackeye Bones brother.

Acknowledgements

A tremendous thank you goes out to anyone and everyone who has shared their time somewhere along the way in the creation of this book. Whether it was bouncing ideas around, or feedback throughout the process, everyone deserves credit for their assistance...

Cover thanks goes to...Ashley Mont
    And...

all of the wonderful Parrotheads who were photographed at Blossom Music Center for a Jimmy Buffett concert that became the group of vacationers for the book...

About the Author...

*M*ike Haszto hails from Islip, New York and continues to live in North Ridgeville, Ohio. He spends most of his time chasing the ever elusive dream of living in paradise...which consists of palm trees, beach on the ocean, and a consistent day weather-wise of sunny and eighty.

Of course, in reality, he spends his time trying to keep up with his children and their activities, and staying active through coaching youth hockey.